Say, Yes Daddy

An ABDL age play romance about a handsome Daddy Dom who introduces his sweet and innocent baby girl to the kinky lifestyle of DDLG

By Tina Moore

Table of Contents

Chapter 1

Thank God it's Friday, Harvey thought as he watched the blonde with the thick ass stretch in front of him. She had been unknowingly teasing him for the last hour, and as her training session came to an end, all Harvey could do was keep his breathing constant as he fought the urge to rip her yoga pants off and bury his aching cock inside of her. *I'd cream-pie this bitch in every hole*, he thought, smiling to himself as he watched her bounce on her toes, her tits jiggling out of her sports bra as she stood, turning to face him.

"Well that's that good session, you worked hard today," Harvey said, wanting to get out of their as fast as he could. The blonde had been getting private training for the last month, and in that time she had done nothing but teased his cock. She had hardly even lost a pound, not that she needed too. She was a fitness model just wanting to maintain her shape in the off-season.

"Thanks, Harvey, see you next week," she said sweetly before walking off, apparently unaware of what he wanted to do to her. Harvey gave a sideward smile as he turned to go to his office. He had set up a private gym at the back of his property, wanting to work for himself after years of working in various gyms around the city. Harvey walked into his office, the air-con hitting him straight away and went to the cage Willow was laying in.

"Get out, I have a job for you," he said, grabbing her by the back of her head and dragging her out. The girl moaned as the vibrator he had stuffed inside of her an hour earlier moved as she crawled on her hands and knees to him. He sat down in his office chair and smiled as her white diapered bottom tried to grind down on the toy he knew was making her cunt leak cum. Harvey placed a hand in his pants and pulled out his hard bulging cock before roughly forcing it into Willow's mouth, her eyes growing wide as his pre-cum ran down the back of her throat.

Willow had been living with Harvey for the last two months, and he had enjoyed keeping her as his fuck doll while he worked, making her be his cum whore in-between clients.

"That's it slut, suck Daddy's big cock. You love that don't you little girl; you love the way Daddy fucks your pretty little mouth. Swallow bitch," Harvey said, taking both of her hands and pinning them behind her back, making her fall back on her heels. Laying on the floor, Harvey sat on her face and watched as the tears began to roll down her face as he dumped his load down her throat, cum spilling out the sides of her mouth.

"Such a pretty little slut," he said, getting off her and walking into the shower. Leaving Willow laying on the floor in the middle of the office alone, his cum still dripping from her lips.

Millie shut her computer down and cracked her neck; it had been a long, hard week. Between her boss's insatiable desire to make her life a living hell and the long-term clients that she lost that week, Millie knew she needed a drink. *6:30*, she thought, looking out the window and breathing in deeply. In the five years, she had worked for the firm; she had never gone home before 6:30. The office was quiet, just the sound of the cleaners starting their shift and Millie wondered what she was doing with her life. Deciding to drop into a bar on her way home to her empty apartment, Millie stood, straightened her A-line pencil skirt and began making her way out of the building.

She passed about four blocks until she found the type of bar she felt comfortable going to. It was quiet, with only a few people sitting inside and most of the lounges free. She walked to the far side of the bar and sat down. From here, she could see who was coming in through the door and sighed as she sipped her drink. Millie took out her phone and began looking through the dating app she had downloaded earlier that week. Disappointed that the men she had matched with were only interested in fucking, she deleted the app and got up, knocking into someone and getting beer over her crisp white blouse.

"Oh I'm so sorry," Millie began gushing as she looked desperately for a napkin. Harvey smiled kindly and took her hand in his, stopping her and causing her to look up at him for the first time. She took in his tall stature, broad shoulders and thick head of hair that was slicked back to one side, his fade-away crisp on the other. Millie held her breath as she saw his dark denim jeans and well-fitting chambray shirt and bit her bottom lip.

"It's ok, I think you might need this more than me anyway," Harvey said, smiling a charmingly wicked smile. Mille smiled meekly, *God his voice is smooth*, she thought accepting the napkin Harvey offered her. Harvey gestured for Millie to sit back down and he re-ordered his beer, pausing to see what she wanted.

"Oh no it's alright," Millie said not wanting to inconvenience Harvey.

"Please?" Harvey said cheekily causing Millie to laugh.

"I'll have what you're having," Millie replied as Harvey placed his hand on the back of her chair. They waited in silence while the bar attender poured the two beers and Millie wondered how she had been so lucky to have such a handsome man turn up to a bar like this one. *Surely he was on his way to a party or something and just came in here for a quiet drink; he's probably just drinking with me because he feels sorry for me*, she thought before thanking the bar attender. Harvey looked over his beer glass at Millie while he drank, winking at her before he put the glass down.

"So, do you always drink by yourself?" He asked, making Millie blush. *Oh, she's cute*, Harvey thought, placing his hand on her thigh, squeezing slightly. Millie was surprised how bold he was being, and it made her cunt ache to be touched instantly.

"Well, no, usually I wouldn't be here at all, but it's Friday, and you know, I just thought maybe I could use a drink," Millie said, stumbling on her words. Harvey just smiled back at her, kindly. *I wonder how this goes down*; he thought as he finished his beer.

"Look, you are so sweet, how about I take you out of this shit-hole, and we go somewhere a little nicer?" He suggested making Millie feel uneasy. She shifted in her seat and tucked her hair behind her ear before looking up at him.

"I don't do that sort of thing," she said, finishing off her beer. Harvey nodded his head understandingly before writing his number down on a napkin.

"Then you'll need this, for when you change your mind," he said making Millie laugh. She watched as Harvey stood up, paid the bar attender and made his way to the door, realizing that she had never even introduced herself or knew his name. She quickly stood and raced after him, grabbing his arm and making him turn around, surprised to be touched so desperately.

"I never introduced myself, I'm Millie," she said, realizing that it was going to be a cold night and that her beer-soaked blouse was making her chest even colder. Harvey took his large brown leather jacket off and draped it over Millie's shoulders.

"Most people call me Harvey," he said, making Millie look confused.

"What do the other people call you?" Millie asked as Harvey pulled the front of the jacket closed on Millie, gently rubbing his thumbs over her hard nipples which were visible through her bra and blouse.

"Daddy," Harvey whispered as he bent down to kiss Millie's cheek before turning on his heel and walking around the corner.

Chapter 2

Harvey had been on her mind all night. Millie had gone home and practically ran to her computer, logging onto her favorite porn site and fucking her desperate cunt for hours. Harvey's jacket still on her shoulders and her arms hurting, she had called it a night by 1:15 in the morning and had fallen asleep in her chair.

Harvey had gone home too, but his night was vastly different from Millie's. He had used Willow like the fuck doll she was, stretching her ass and filling it with as much cum as it would take before diapering her and chaining her to his bed.

"Hi, is this Harvey?" Millie asked into her phone the next morning. She hadn't been able to fight the urge to call him. She needed to hear his smooth, sexy voice again.

"Yes, it is Miss Millie. How are you?" Harvey

replied as calm as ever. Millie giggled hearing the way Harvey was speaking with her, and she involuntarily rubbed herself over her fluffy pajama shorts. Although it was the middle of winter, the heating in Millie's apartment made it feel like spring, and she enjoyed being able to wear her short shorts and tight white racer back singlet around the house.

"I was just ringing to see when I can return your jacket to you," Millie said, her voice going high.

"No, you're not. Your call has nothing to do with my jacket, tell me why you are calling," Harvey said, sounding slightly more severe. Millie swallowed hard as she felt her body betray her, and her panties get wet.

"I want to see you again," Millie said softly. Harvey leaned back; he had been sitting in bed, slapping Willow's open mouth with his cock until now. He got up and enjoyed that Willow had to stay in bed as he began to rub his hardening cock in front of her.

"When are you free?" Harvey said, trying to keep his breathing constant. Millie giggled.

"I'm free tonight?" She said, hoping that Harvey would agree. Harvey stroked his cock through his large hands, shaking it slightly and watched as Willow turned around obediently. Harvey climbed back up into bed and placed Willow's panties in her mouth before he slipped the tip of his cock into her soft, pink pussy.

"Tonight would be perfect. Let's meet at our bar, and we can go from there. Say 7?" Harvey said, reaching around and rubbing Willow's clit, making her shake her hips on him.

"7 would be perfect, see you then," Millie said making Harvey smile and end the call as he plunged into Willow's ready cunt.

"Daddy's got a date tonight baby girl, do you know what that means?" Harvey said, throwing the phone onto the bed and placing both his hands on Willow's motherly hips. He pumped aggressively in and out of her making her moan and dip her head in submission as he nailed her.

"No? Ok, let Daddy tell you then. It means that Uncle Ben is going to come over and take care of you. And I'm going to leave you dirty and used so that if he wants you, he'll have to fuck you over the top of Daddy's cum, so you know that I'm always there. Would you like that baby girl? My little whore," Harvey said, feeling Willow's juices break inside of her and gush out around his cock.

"Yeah, I thought so," Harvey laughed, slapping her ass dismissingly before he pulled out of her and came on her back.

"Come here, jam jams time," Harvey said unchaining Willow and pulling up her purple onesie over her used body. Harvey held her in his arms.

"Will you be a good girl for Daddy and let Uncle Ben play with you the way he wants baby girl?" Harvey asked Willow, who was smiling widely and nodding her head. Willow liked to be taken a lot rougher than Harvey would have usually wanted to give, but she had been thrown out of her last Daddy's house after she broke a rule he had. Harvey had thought it was stupid of him to not just punish her for it, throwing her out seemed a bit extreme and such a waste. She had contacted Harvey asking if she could stay a few nights while she sorted out getting a new apartment, but things had moved fast. With Harvey fucking her on the first night and he had let her stay with the knowledge that their relationship was not ever going to be long-lasting. Willow had understood that Harvey didn't want a girl like her who wanted to be used so viciously and share, but she still enjoyed having him for as long as she had.

Willow nodded her head and gasped as Harvey pulled her panties out of her mouth.

"Yes, Daddy," she replied, receiving a gentle slap on her face as Harvey got up to get ready for the day.

"Hi," Millie said, enjoying how Harvey looked at her the minute their eyes met. She had taken her time getting ready tonight, deciding on a soft pink dress with white stockings and pink heels. Her blonde hair was down, and her blue eyes sparkled as the lights of the bar reflected in them. Harvey was not the only impressed one, as the eyes of the other men in the dive of a bar continued to steal long, lustful stares at the 24-year-old.

"Howdy," Harvey replied, kissing her on the top of her head and gesturing to the bar attender to pour two beers. Millie couldn't help herself and brought her arms up to hug Harvey's waist, enjoying the feel of his big belt buckle pressing against her tummy.

"How have you been sweetie?" Harvey said, stroking her hair before sitting down. He took off his dark grey felt coat and began to roll up the sleeves of his oxford cotton button down, showing off his muscular forearms. Millie hadn't realized she had been staring until he cleared his throat and tilted his head slightly.

"Oh I've been fine, um, here," Millie said, snapping herself back into reality and passing Harvey his jacket. He smiled, accepting it again and hung it over the back of the bar stool. She nervously began to tear at the cuticles of her manicured hands, making her nail slightly bleed.

"Baby girl, you hurt yourself," Harvey involuntarily said, frowning and reaching into his jeans pocket, to Millie's surprise, pulling out a plaster.

"Here," Harvey said lovingly, catching Millie off guard. She watched in awe as Harvey gently took her hand in his and placed the plaster over her finger.

"There, all better, no more of that," he said, making her blush and pull away from him, looking down at the princess plaster he had just put over her finger.

"Great, no I look like I'm a little girl," Millie laughed, holding up her finger to show him. Harvey just smiled a knowing smile and leaned back in his stool, picked up his beer, and took a sip.

"Aren't you?" He said smirking when Millie raised an eyebrow at him.

"Um, no!" She exclaimed, looking herself up

and down. Harvey just placed his hand on her cheek and stroked it with his thumb.

"Well, that's not what I see, baby girl," he replied before gesturing that they should leave the bar.

"Where do you want to go?" Millie said, standing up and reaching for her coat that Harvey already had in his hands.

"Turn around," he said kindly making Millie roll her eyes dramatically before following his instructions. Harvey wasn't like the guys she had had before. They had all been jerks who treated her like she was just something to brag about. But Harvey was handsome and gentle and made her feel like she could never be hurt again. She cursed herself for feeling so obsessed with him when it was only the first time they were spending any time together.

"Let's go, baby," Harvey said, holding out his hand to her. She playful pushed it away before walking confidently out of the bar in front of him. He smiled at his feet and walked out after her, quickly grabbing her by her upper arm and pulling her back to him.

"Hold Daddy's hand, baby girl," he said while his other hand snaked its way around her waist. Millie swallowed hard and bit the side of her bottom lip as she felt Harvey's hard cock press into the back of her dress. She stayed there, letting him softly grope at her before he turned her around and looked at her deep in her eyes.

"Just let me know if you want to stop, ok?" Harvey said, bending down and kissing the tip of her nose. Millie nodded her head and wrapped both her arms around his large arm as they waited for a taxi.

Harvey took Millie to a family owned Mexican restaurant down a small side alley, and Millie had been blown away that he would know somewhere so quaint and magical. They talked about art and what their dreams where both laughing that they thought working a 9-5 was a ridiculous waste of life and Millie reached for Harvey's hand as they walked back out onto the street.

"Harvey, I've had a charming time," Millie said. Harvey looked down to see she was smiling up at him, her big blue eyes catching the moonlight.

"I'm glad you have little one. Do you have space in there for one more thing?" Harvey said, walking them over to a park bench and sitting her on his lap. Millie was surprised how relaxed she was with him as she rested her head on his broad chest and nodded sleepily up at him.

"Good," Harvey said, unbuckling his belt and subtly reaching under Millie's dress. She gasped as she felt his hand in her stockings, pressing on her slit and holding her firmer when he found how wet she was. Millie could feel his cock getting hard again, bulging between her thighs and pushing into her.

"Can Daddy fill you up, baby girl?" Harvey said lifting Millie slightly and repositioning his thick cock, ready to bury it up his sweet date. Millie just nodded as Harvey gently reached both hands under her dress and pulled her stockings down, before lifting her and placing her down onto his erect shaft, making her take it all at once as he lowered her back onto him. Millie squirmed at the size of the cock filling her, unsure if it was too big for her to take and waited for her muscles to relax around the monster that had invaded her.

"Daddy, I," was all Millie could say before Harvey covered her mouth with his hand and wrapped his other one around her waist.

"You said you still had room, little one," he teased, keeping still as not to hurt her. He felt Millie clench her cunt around his cock, and he placed his hands on both sides of her ass, lifting her again before letting her drop down from a couple of inches from his lap.

"Good thing no one is around to hear your little moans, baby girl," Harvey laughed as he repeated his actions, forcing Millie to take him harder and harder. Millie just placed her hands on his knees, bending forward and feeling him deeper inside of her.

"I can't," Millie said, struggling to get down from Harvey's lap, wanting his huge cock out of her. He helped her, lifting her and off him and placing her gently on her shaking legs, quickly catching her as her legs gave way underneath her. Putting his still hard cock back in his pants, Harvey held Millie in his arms, wrapping his opened coat around her as her breathing returned to normal.

"Are you alright, baby girl? Teddy is quite greedy, but he likes filling up your pretty princess parts. Next time maybe he'll fill you up with his Teddy cream too," Harvey said, stroking his cock over his jeans. Millie didn't know what came over her, but she began to suck her thumb as he cuddled her, watching him stroke down his hard erection.

"Teddy?" She softly asked Harvey, who just nodded. He took her hand and placed it over the pole that was kept down by his tight jeans making her stroke it for him.

"Teddy is clever, he can make you scream and giggle at the same time," Harvey replied, making Millie giggle before going back to sucking her thumb.

"Come on baby, let's get you home," he added, reaching under Millie's skirt and putting her panties and stockings back in place before taking her free hand and walking her back out onto the main road.

Chapter 3

"Willow, do you want milk with your coffee?" Harvey said three days later. He had known that he needed to cut her loose the minute he speared Millie with his cock. He found her willingness to be taken and used was so perfectly complimented by her sweet femininity that he couldn't imagine not having her in his life. Millie had messaged him daily, asking him all the questions a new date would. They had shared their childhood stories, how they had chosen their careers, and what they looked for in a partner. Millie had explained that she had never been with a guy who called himself Daddy and Harvey sent her a few internet links for her to read different articles about the DDlg kink. He was relieved that she had messaged back saying that she wasn't sure if she wanted all that the kink covered but that she liked what they had done so far.

"Yeah, of course, I do," Willow replied, looking over her laptop annoyed that he had asked. Harvey rolled his eyes and took the milk jug in one hand and the morning paper in the other. He sat down, deciding that today would be the day he let her go. He had contemplated how he should do it; he had no feelings for the woman but still didn't want just to throw her out, ending the relationship like her last one.

"Wills, it's that time," Harvey said, placing the paper on the table and pouring the milk into her coffee cup. Willow looked her green eyes up without moving her head.

"You look like a demon like that," Harvey smirked watching her face. She lifted her head and sipped her coffee.

"She's that good is she?" Willow teased getting up and kissing Harvey's cheek as she passed, going into the kitchen and taking down the cereal before walking back to the table.

"Yeah, she is," he replied flicking through his phone looking at the photos Millie had just sent him. She was sitting on the floor, on her knees, her soft thighs open, light blue lace panties covering her creamy white pussy. The photo was cut off at her nipples, and he liked how innocent she was. Putting his phone away, Harvey looked back up at Willow who was busy typing on her keyboard.

"So, let's look for a place you can move into?" He suggested flicking through the paper to the real estate section.

"Already on it," Willow said, smiling, turning the laptop around and coming to sit on his lap. He knew what she was doing and reached around to rub her naked pussy.

"You're such a fucking slut Willow," he laughed, pushing his two fingers into her roughly making her bend forward and gasp as he pounded her knuckle deep.

"Thank you, Harvey," she breathlessly panted, aware that he was giving her what she wanted.

"It's ok sweetie, cum for me and then we need to find you someone who will look after this little cunt the way you need it," Harvey said holding her down by her neck and pulling his fingers from her cumming pussy. He reached into his pants and pressed the tip of his cock into her ass, taking her by surprise.

"Take it, bitch, don't you dare fucking refuse me," Harvey growled slapping her ass and thighs until she relaxed and let him slide into her, stretching her as he gently jerked his cock inside her, his cum squirting into her. Pulling out, he went to the kitchen drawer and rolled on a condom.

"Get down here," he said snapping his fingers to the couch and taking Willow's wrist in his large hand and threw her down before getting on his knees and stabbing her wet pussy with his long thick cock fucking the air out of her lungs.

"Willow, it'll be alright," Harvey said as tears began to roll down her cheeks. He stood up, careful to keep his cock buried deep inside her and lifted her, holding her in his arms as she was fucked. He took her arms and held them behind her back as his other arm held her up, bouncing her up and down on his rod, forcing her to be fucked slightly beyond her limit. He knew that he was just over the line by her limp submission, her head resting on his shoulder, his chest wet with her tears.

"I've got you, you're ok," Harvey said lovingly. He kissed the top of her head before letting go of her arms and feeling them flying around his neck as he continued to force long strokes inside her, hitting her hilt and pushing into her. Feeling his cock push her tummy out. Her muscles destroyed.

"That's enough sweetie," he said, flicking cum onto the wooden floor as he lifted her off the pulsing cock that just fucked her to exhaustion. He lowered her onto the sofa and went into his bedroom, collecting a packet of wet wipes and her blanket. Walking back into the kitchen, he filled her sippy cup with warm milk and found her pink chew toy before he came back by her side and sat on the floor next to the sofa as he wiped down her dripping cunt. He took out a new wipe and wiped her face, kissing the tip of her nose and cupping her face in both his hands.

"No more little one," Harvey said, looking into Willow's wide eyes, her head nodding as Harvey began to tuck the blanket around her shivering body. He passed her the sippy cup and patted her tummy as she drank, her eyes closing and her smaller hands resting on top of his.

"What happened to you?" Harvey said, knowing that she was trying to fuck away some deeply, set in pain that someone had done to her.

"No Harvey," was all Willow replied, knowing that there was no way to explain the pain she was feeling, that she hadn't even let herself explore it to understand what it was that harmed her so powerfully. Harvey just nodded and stroked her forehead as she passed him back her empty milk cup and began chewing on the pink teething ring that she had successfully torn apart in one selection.

"I'll get you a new one before you go,"

Harvey said frowning at how damaged she had made her current one.

"I can do that myself, Harvey. I'm grateful to you, really, but it is ok, you don't have to care for me anymore," Willow said smiling a genuine smile, her hard eyes softening for a moment before turning cold again.

Millie had read up on the DDlg kink for days, getting turned on watching different porn videos and realizing that there was a whole new world that she hadn't ever considered exploring before. She wondered how Harvey had found it and had just short of 50 thousand questions she wanted to ask him. Delighted when he rang shortly after she had sent a slight cock tease of a photo, she picked up more quickly than she usually would have.

"Hi," Millie excitedly said down the phone, causing Harvey to laugh involuntarily.

"Hey sweetie, what are you up to?" Harvey said, sitting in the hammock outside on the back porch. From his position, he over-looked the downward slope, which leads to the pond. He had introduced ducks to the lake two years ago and watched as they swam around dipping their head under the water as Millie told him all the things she had done in the last three days.

"Wow, baby girl sounds like you've been busy! Of course, I can answer your questions, do you want to meet up somewhere a little more private so we can talk openly?" Harvey suggested, looking up at the white clouds that scattered across the sky.

"Sure, where are you thinking?" Millie asked. Harvey thought for a moment before placing his hand on his cock, playing with his balls as he spoke.

"Want to come over and see my house?" He asked, a cheeky grin spreading across his face. Millie laughed.

"You just want to play Harvey!" She accused, and Harvey gave a sideward smile.

"Now look, if I wanted to play, do you think I wouldn't just take you when and where I wanted to? Didn't I spread your thighs and push Teddy deep inside you the minute I wanted to last time?" Harvey said, his cock hardening under his grey sweat pants as he spoke the words that made Millie gasp, her cunt aching instantly.

"Yeah, I guess you did," she replied, wondering where the conversation would go.

"And didn't I stop the minute you wanted to?" He added, smiling at himself as he felt like such a good guy for doing the only thing he should have.

"Yeah," Millie said cautiously.

"Well, I guess you can trust me then sweetheart can't you?" Harvey asked, remembering how tight Millie was, how his 8 inches almost didn't fit.

"I'll send you my address, let me know how long it takes you and when you are on your way little one, Daddy wants to make sure I've set up our afternoon tea spread in time," Harvey said as he slowly jerked off before hanging up the phone. He got up out of the hammock and took his shirt off, letting it fall onto the grass and as he pulled his designer sweats down slightly as he jerked off in the privacy of his expansive back yard.

"Fuck this is good," Harvey moaned as he shot his load onto the grass, happy to be able to be so free. He laughed to himself as he put his cock back into his pants, enjoying the feeling of the soft material against his wet rod, bent down to pick up his white T-shirt and headed back inside to find that Willow had gone to his bedroom.

"I'm going to have company Willow, is there something you can do for tonight?" Harvey said, throwing his clothes into the wash basket and stepping into the shower.

"Will?" He asked when no reply came. Willow took her earphones from her ears and looked at him, confused.

"Huh?" She asked, walking into the bathroom and watched as Harvey washed his chiseled body. He ran his soapy hands over his rippled abs, his side tattoo moving as his muscles flex when he reached around his back.

"Have you got something to do tonight? I'm having a guest," Harvey said, repeating himself and letting the water run over his head before he shook his hair and leaned back against the shower wall.

"Oh, yeah, no trouble. I'll be gone all weekend if that's cool," Willow said, biting her lip as she watched Harvey run his fingers through his hair.

"Good," he said, turning around, dismissing her. Willow tightened her pussy as she turned and walked away, racking her brain as to what she could spend her weekend doing.

Chapter 4

"Well hello there precious," Harvey said, opening the door seeing Millie kneeling in front of him. She had obliviously dropped her handbag, the contents sprawled out over the front steps.

"Let me help you, little lady," he added, bending down and helping her pick up her things. Millie blushed and looked at him sheepishly before clearing her throat.

"Hi Daddy," she softly said, biting her lip, hoping that she was saying the right thing.

"Oh baby," Harvey said scooping Millie up with one arm and picking her bag up with the other as he carried her into his house. Millie gasped as she saw the country style house, the dark timber wooden floors, and cowhide in the living room, the big fireplace and smelt the vanilla and berry scented candles.

"Wow," was all Millie could say as she was

caught off guard by Harvey's sophisticated and stylish home.

"I'm glad you like it," Harvey whispered in Millie's ear, gently lowering her to the floor, making sure she was settled on her feet before he let her go entirely.

"I'll just put your bag over here sweetie," Harvey said, placing her bag next to the sofa before taking her hand and leading her through the house to the back porch. He had set up fairy cakes and tea and coffee over the white linen table cloth on the whitewashed wooden table that overlooked the pond.

"Harvey," was all Millie could say becoming overwhelmed with the beauty of his home.

"No baby, I'm Daddy," Harvey tenderly said, pulling the chair out for Millie who absent-mindedly sat and nodded.

"Yes, Daddy," she answered as Harvey sat next to her and offered her coffee.

"Um no, may I have tea please?" Millie asked, pulling herself away from the view and looking into Harvey's sparkling brown eyes. Harvey put the coffee jug down and placed his hand gently on Millie's cheek, pushing his thumb into her mouth, happy she didn't resist him.

"Say, please Daddy," Harvey prompted, enjoying having a new baby to teach.

"Please Daddy," Millie said around Harvey's thick thumb. He kept it in her mouth as he poured her the tea.

"When Daddy puts something in your mouth baby girl, I want you to suck it until I take it out, alright?" Harvey said, watching as Millie's lips form a pout around his thumb as she began to obey his instruction.

"Good girl baby Millie," Harvey said, feeling her tongue stroke him as she sucked.

"Clever girl. You're going to be a good girl for Daddy won't you," Harvey said as he reached out to grope Millie's massive breasts. He liked that she had a small frame and large fuck-able tits. *She's going to be perfect, her tits are so full and ripe, they are going to look so good bound, and cock fucked,*

Harvey thought getting hard under the table. Taking his thumb out of her mouth, he smiled lovingly and placed a cake on her plate.

"So, what do you want to know?" Harvey asked biting the wings off his cake and wiping the cream that stayed on his bottom lip with his index finger before sticking it in Millie's mouth, getting aroused by how her full lips looked with his thick finger stuffed in her little mouth.

"Oh, baby is a quick learner," Harvey said excitedly as Millie sucked his finger deep into her throat. Harvey waited longer than he needed to before taking his finger from her lips.

"Like, do you like all this sort of stuff?" Millie said, reaching for her phone and beginning to flick through wanting to show him the photos she had saved. Harvey took her photo and put it on the other side of the table.

"Use your words little one," he said, making Millie blush as she tried to form the words she had never spoken in this context before.

"Like, diapers and stuff," she said, trying to

hide her embarrassment. Harvey sat back and enjoyed her discomfort before handing her the phone again.

"Yes, I like dressing my partner in diapers and stuff," he teased using her words as he let her find the photos.

"Like this?" Millie asked, showing him the album she had created. He flicked through the photos of women in diapers and onesies, the ones with pacifiers in their mouths and Daddies who had stuff their cocks into the diaper covered pussies of their babies. He stopped on a photo of a woman in a pink dress, her pink diaper showing as she was bent over an older man's lap and spanked. Her legs were bound, and her arms were cuffed behind her back as a vibrator had been pushed into her pussy, and a dildo was used to gag her.

"Do you like the idea of this?" Harvey asked, raising an eyebrow at Millie, knowing that anything he said or did with her, would make her feel humiliated in lustful shame.

"Yes, Daddy," Millie softly said, biting her

bottom lip. Harvey saw that she hadn't eaten her cake and he took a fork and broke off a piece for her, feeding her the mouthful as her eyes went wide as she opened her mouth.

"I think you are going to love being mine sweetheart. Daddy is going to treat you real good," Harvey said, kissing her lips, parting them with his tongue, tasting her vanilla bean frosting covered tongue. He moaned as he got up, knocking his chair backward as he kicked it away and lifted Millie into his arms. He took her chin in his hand, holding her mouth to his as he walked down to the hammock, all the while tasting her and feeling her grind into his waist. Harvey lay down on the hammock and placed Millie on top of him, feeling the weight of her heavy tits and hard nipples through her tight printed T-shirt. Harvey carefully grabbed a fistful of her hair, pulling her head backward slowly and looking into her eyes. Millie placed her hands on his chest, and he liked how it felt as she pushed against him and sat up, straddling his lap, her knees up like a little frog.

Her short flowy skirt had fallen back, exposing her puffy pussy pressing hard against light pink cotton panties, the subtle line of her wetness making Harvey's fingers reach up to touch her.

"God you are so beautiful Millie," Harvey said, pulling her panties to the side and stroking her up and down her wet slit, feeling the small bud of her clit hot under his touch. He continued to stroke her as she began to grind against his fingers, resting both her hands on his chest, her tits being squeezed between her arms. She could feel him as she slowly dry humped his camel colored trousers enjoying his hardening bulge pushing into her ass, his fingers only adding to her frustration.

"Tell Daddy what you want, baby girl," Harvey said bucking his hips making Millie bounce on his fingers, being touched deeper than she had been prepared for, her gasp as he entered her without warning making her eyes go wide.

"Please fuck me, Daddy," Millie said desperately, grinding down hard on Harvey's fingers as they began to slowly wiggle inside of her, his thumb flicking her clit in time with his slow onslaught. Millie moaned and closed her eyes as he edged her closer to orgasm. Harvey licked his lip before reaching into his pants and pulling out his erect cock, rubbing his full balls.

"Not yet, baby girl," he whispered, sitting up and taking his fingers from Millie who whimpered in frustration only adding to his arousal.

"What do I have to do to get fucked, Daddy?" Millie said involuntarily as she grabbed his cock and began jerking him off. Harvey laughed and took her hands away, making Millie confused as to why he was rejecting her touch.

"Those are some very big words young lady," Harvey teased, enjoying having Millie a hot mess ready to do whatever he asked.

"You haven't finished your cake yet sweetie, I can't have that little tummy of yours empty," Harvey said as he jerked himself off, rubbing his cock up and down Millie's slit.

"Then fill me with Teddy," Millie said, bending her head and licking his balls. Harvey pushed himself into her mouth, placing his hand on the back of her head and forcing both his cum filled balls into her mouth until she gagged. His pre-cum dripping onto Millie's cheek as she sucked his heavy sack.

"Suck Daddy like a good girl," Harvey said, pushing her head down and pushing his balls down her throat, moaning as he felt her gag around them.

"You surprise me, baby girl," Harvey said, slapping his rock hard cock against Millie's face. Millie could feel the fresh air of the afternoon turning into night as her ass wiggled in the air, spit dribbling from her lips and onto Harvey's trousers. Her skirt had fallen to rest on her back, her bubble butt jiggling much to Harvey's delight as he thrust into her mouth. Suddenly feeling her head being pulled back, Harvey wiped the saliva from her chin and turned her around, so she was facing away from him.

"Let's warm you up a little bit," Harvey said, pulling the side of Millie's panties up on the side of her ass and pushing his cock along her ass crack. He held her hips in his hands, licking his lips as he saw how she looked having his cock rubbing up and down her soft skin. Slapping Millie's hands away when she tried to reach for his cock, Harvey began trusting more feverishly against her skin, his wet balls slapping against the side of her ass as he came hard, his load dripping down into her ass crack, pooling at her ass-hole.

"Daddy made a mess, baby girl, let's see if I can tidy you up," Harvey said rubbing his oozing cock up and down her slit, covering her, claiming her cunt as his. He bent over her, reaching for her tits, pulling on them like he was milking her as his cock rested under her panties at the top of her ass.

"If anything is ever too much, you need to tell Daddy red ok, baby? I don't ever want to do something you don't like, that's not fun for me," Harvey said pulling on Millie's nipples and flicking them as the first stars began to flicker across the open sky.

"Yes, Daddy. What do I say if I want you to smash my cunt?" Millie asked feeling cheeky and hornier than she had ever in her life. Harvey laughed and placed both his hands on the back of Millie's panties and slowly pulled them down, moving her thighs together and pushing her head down.

"You say, please Daddy," Harvey said pushing his cock past Millie's soft, puffy pussy lips and straight into her cunt, her panties forcing her knees together and his thighs pinning her body down. Millie moaned and tried to buck her ass back but was only met with another powerful thrust of Harvey's hips, spearing her aching cunt but this time he kept it inside of her loving how her muscles tighten around his cock as it intruded into her most precious place.

"If you want, little girl, Daddy will make you his," Harvey said, placing his hands on her wrists and holding them down in front of her, stretching her arms forward.

"Please, Daddy," Millie moaned as though she was breathing for the first time. Harvey pulled out just to force himself inside her again, her legs beginning to shake. He fucked her balls deep, enjoying how his orgasm started to build in time with Millie's. Deciding that he wanted to surprise Millie with one more tease, Harvey got up and pulled out of her abruptly making her whine in frustration of her orgasm denial.

"Daddy doesn't care if you cum or not baby girl. Your pussy is for my enjoyment, not yours. If you cum, lucky you, but if you don't, don't complain to Daddy," Harvey said getting out of the hammock, his need to cum so intense it was almost painful.

"Yes, Daddy," Millie said as he repositioned her so that she was on all fours, facing the pond, her dripping pussy glistening in the moonlight as Harvey positioned himself behind her, pushing his cold, cum-covered cock back into her warm cunt. He grabbed her hips and buried himself deep inside her, pushing her hips away, making her swing on the hammock before coming back only for her pussy to be pierced by Harvey's pulsing shaft. Her pussy lips splitting as Millie's pussy gobbled up Harvey's cock with each swing back, her hilt being hit time after time.

"Stay like that, sweetie," Harvey said slapping Millie's ass lovingly as he saw her arms begin to shake as the hammock swung back, again forcing her pussy to take Harvey's cumming cock, being squirted with his cream each time he filled her. Her cunt quickly taking all of him, his balls full and soft against her ass as he held the hammock in place and pushed them into her. Holding the hammock in place with one hand, Harvey reached around and grabbed the front of Millie's throat as he began to pound her powerfully, feeling her cum squirt against his cock, feeling his cum mixing inside of her and spilling from her hole and down her thighs. Tightening his grip, he felt Millie gasp for air just as he pulled out his now limp cock. He pushed Millie down on the hammock as her breaths came in shallow gasps, and her pussy juices still pouring from her as she lay spent. The hammock swung gently in the night breeze as Harvey sat back on the grass, catching his breath. He heard Millie's breath return to normal and watched as she cautiously looked over the top of the hammock to stare at him.

"Are you ok, baby girl? Did Daddy hurt you at all?" Harvey said as Millie just shook her head, despite the tears that were being to fall from her eyes.

"Oh, baby, what is it?" Harvey said as he stood quickly, worried he had hurt her.

"I have never been fucked like that before," Millie said as he cupped her face in his hands. Harvey just smiled as he saw Millie work through her space, reaching into the hammock to pick her up and began to carry her back to the house.

"Daddy likes carrying you like a princess," Harvey said, placing Millie down on his bed. He gently rolled her panties the rest of the way down her legs, took off her skirt, T-shirt, and bra, getting a surprise when he saw her nipples where pierced.

"Naughty little girl!" Harvey exclaimed, marveling at how pink her nipples were. The piercing bars forcing her nipples to stay hard, the large buds looking like buttons Harvey knew he wanted to tease all over again. Millie saw the desire in his eyes.

"You can if you want Daddy," she said, her little voice surprising her as she heard it for the first time. It didn't escape Harvey either, and he took in her form. Her body was soft, the thin layer of untoned tummy over her abs jiggling when he placed his hand on her and patted her gently.

"You are such a good girl for Daddy, but I think you've had enough sweetie," Harvey said, making Millie smile and close her eyes, exhausted psychologically as well as physically. Harvey took his navy cable knit sweater off, his white T-shirt clinging to his bulk mass. He peeled it off, followed by his trousers and picked everything up before placing it in the washing basket.

"Come to Daddy little miss, let's get you all cleaned up," Harvey said, picking up Millie, realizing that she had fallen asleep.

"Huh?" Millie said, opening her eyes and looking around, turning her body slightly in Harvey's arms as he held her while the bath water ran. He lit scented candles and added bath salts to the warm water of the spa bath before carefully stepping in with Millie still in his arms. Sitting down in the water, Millie snuggled into his chest, and he poured coconut and shea butter body lotion over Millie's tits, soaping her up in a thick lather, letting her tits bounce out of his hands, pulling them back up by her nipples as she sleepily rested in his arms. Taking his time to rub her cunt, not wanting to hurt her and understanding how sensitive she still was by how swollen she still was.

"Daddy, can I please stay the night?" Millie suddenly asked, turning to look up at him, her wide eyes looking at him innocently causing his heart to flutter.

"Yes, baby girl. Daddy wasn't going to let you go tonight, don't worry," Harvey said, pouring warm water over her body, rinsing her off.

"But are you going to be a good girl and let Daddy dress you?" Harvey asked, wondering how far she would let him go. Millie just nodded her head, deep in the little space she hadn't realized was too close to the surface.

"Come on then, the water is starting to get a cold little one," Harvey said, taking Millie by the hand and leading her out of the bath. He took down a fluffy black towel and dried her off, kissing her softly as he patted the water droplets off her body.

"Take Daddy's hand," Harvey said and waited for Millie to obey before walking her back to his bed.

"Lay down little one," he instructed, watching as Millie lowered herself on top of his sheets, her body being swallowed up by the marshmallow-like quilt and pillows. Harvey took out baby powder, a bunny print diaper and doubled the lining he usually would have used. He placed them down on the bed before going back to the cupboard and opening up a draw of onesies.

He chose a baby pink long sleeved onesies that had a bunny print on the front to match the diaper he was going to put Millie in and a black pacifier. He took out black thigh high socks and walked back to the bed.

"Alright little girl, let's get you ready for bed," Harvey said grabbing Millie by her hips and pulling her body down to the edge of the bed and towards his cock which to Millie's surprise was hard again.

"Daddy I don't think I can," Millie said, bringing her hands to cover her pussy, thinking that Harvey was going to fuck her again. He laughed and leaned over her, his cock pressing into her hands as he kissed her face all over.

"Teddy isn't going to play with you again little one, don't worry, he knows when you can't play anymore," Harvey said taking her hands away and placing them above her head. He took the diaper and gently slapped Millie's thighs.

"Lift your bottom, baby," he instructed and waited for Millie to follow his direction. He placed the diaper under her bottom, enjoying her surprised face at how it felt. He placed a hand on her chest as she tried to rest on her elbows, pushing her back down.

"Stay still for Daddy," he said, moving his hands, making her tits to jiggle as she felt the powered sprinkle over her pussy for the first time. He pulled the diaper tight, the thickness of the padding soft against her sensitive pussy.

"Such a pretty girl," Harvey said, taking the onesie and pulling it over Millie's head and wriggling it down her body, enjoying how she looked rolling around the bed in her diaper. Millie giggled as Harvey took her wrists in his hands and pulled her arms into the sleeves of the soft outfit.

"One last thing," Harvey said, pushing the pacifier into Millie's mouth, slapping her cheek gently when she tried to refuse him.

"Don't be bad for Daddy little girl," Harvey said, running his hands over Millie's thickly diapered pussy. Millie moaned behind her paci and wriggled against Harvey's touch as he tickled her all over.

"Daddy stop it," Millie giggled, her little voice making Harvey lick his lips. He got up and pulled on his long pajama sweats before climbing in bed with Millie.

"Come and cuddle Daddy," he said, pulling her to him, patting her between her splayed thighs as she began to fall asleep.

Chapter 5

"Who is a pretty baby?" Willow said brushing Millie's hair back, stroking her forehead. Millie opened her sleepy eyes and was startled by the black haired woman lying next to her.

"Shh little girl, it is ok," Willow said, pulling Millie into her arms, easily overpowering a resisting Millie. Forgetting she had a paci in her mouth, Millie tried to speak but as her words came out as incoherent mumble, making Willow laughed cruelly.

"Oh sweetie, I don't understand your baby talk," Willow said, placing her hand over the top of Millie's mouth making holding her head in place.

"What? Don't you want a Mama as well as a Daddy little girl?" Willow teased, wrapping her legs around Millie's and forcing them open as she rubbed Millie's diaper covered pussy. Millie tried to look for Harvey but couldn't see him.

"Daddy has gone out little girl; he won't be back for a while. Guess you will have to stay with Mama until he gets back," Willow said cruelly as she stroked Millie.

"Didn't he tell you about me little one?" Willow said, looking down to see Millie's tear-filled eyes. Millie shook her head but settled into Willow's arms. Feeling another woman's breasts for the first time, as Willow pressed herself against Millie's face.

"Well that was rude of him," Willow said annoyed that she hadn't been given a mention.

"Regardless, if I let you go, will you be a good girl for Mama?" Willow said. Millie took in the dark beauty of the woman who had so boldly forced herself on her and felt silly for being so naïve. *Of course, he already has a girlfriend*, Millie thought sadly, but she just nodded her head and looked down, embarrassed to be dressed like this in front of the stunningly attractive and powerful woman. Willow placed both her hands on the side of Millie's cheeks and softened more than she realized she could as she thumbed away the tears that fell from Millie's eyes.

"Shh baby, it's ok, Mama is going to take care of you," Willow said, kissing Millie's cheeks before taking the paci from Millie's mouth.

"There, little Millie, what a sweet girl you are," Willow said, smiling kindly at Millie.

"Um, I think I should go," Millie softly said, trying to get up. Willow sat back and watched as Millie began to take her onesie off, pulling at the clips between her legs, her fingers fumbling to get them open. Willow rolled her eyes and placed her hands over the top of Millie's.

"Let Mama," Willow said, pushing Millie onto her back. Millie breathed deeply as Willow ripped the clips open in one quick motion and began running her hands up Millie's body, pulling the onesie off as she went. Stopping just under Millie's big tits, Willow bent down and kissed Millie's soft tummy making Millie tighten her abs and try to pull away from Willow.

"You'll have to get used to Mama touching

you little one. Have you ever been touch by a woman before?" Willow asked, the answer already evident by the reluctant consent Millie was giving her. Millie shook her head no, unable to speak as Willow decided to keep Millie's tits covered. She came to lay next to Millie once again, this time making Millie's eyes go wide as she was frozen by what she saw. Willow unzipped her black bomber jacket exposing her E-cup natural looking but fake tits nestled in a dark red lace bra. Millie watched, almost captivated as Willow let her coat fall to the side, never breaking eye contact with Millie as she reached around and unhooked her bra.

"Do you like what you see little girl, are you hungry for Mama?" Willow asked, pulling the bottom of Millie's onesie back down and doing the clips up again.

"Uh uh little girl, don't get fussy for Mama," Willow said as Millie reached down and tried to push her hands away. Willow stared Millie down with her piercing green eyes until Millie took her hands away, her head spinning by having another woman treat her like this. Willow moved up to the head of the bed and sat against it, patting her lap seductively.

"Come here, princess," she cooed, excited to have Millie obey her so willingly. Millie lay down on Willow's lap, facing up and looking into Willow's captivating eyes, opening her mouth involuntarily as Willow bent forward and rubbed her nipple across Millie's lips.

"What did Daddy teach you little one?" Willow said, stroking Millie's tummy before patting her diapered pussy.

"To suck whatever he put in my mouth," Millie said quietly making Willow smile.

"Then open wide bubba," Willow said. Millie parted her lips just as she felt Willow's nipple pressing into her mouth and began sucking the older woman's nipple. Willow moaned at how soft Millie's tongue was and bent her knees up to roll Millie into her, patting her ass and uncovered thighs.

"Such a good girl," Willow said, surprised at

how loving she felt towards Millie. *This was not the fucking plan*; she thought to herself as she moved her arm to cradle Millie who continued to suckle from her. Enjoying a tender moment with Millie, Willow stroked her cheek as she sucked, smiling lovingly at Millie when she made little noises. Millie was surprised she liked what was happening to her, and she brought her hands up to hold Willow's heavy breast in her hands. Willow bent down to kiss Millie's forehead in delighted bliss as she saw how Millie's hands looked small on her tit and repositioned herself, so Millie didn't have to hold the weight of it all herself.

"We have such sweet girl," Willow said victoriously as she looked up and saw Harvey walking towards the open bedroom door. He was carrying a shopping bag and placed it at the entrance of the room as he looked in. Rage was the first emotion he felt. Anger that Willow was holding his baby girl, rage at whatever she had done to convince Millie to be in that position. He knew it couldn't have been Millie's fault; she was sweet and new and innocent. Willow, on the other hand, he knew to be wicked. Harvey came and sat next to Willow and looked down into Millie's eyes. He smiled at her before kissing her on her nose, deciding that it was better to punish Willow in private, he didn't want to scare Millie off by what he was already planning to do to Willow.

"She is a good girl, aren't you, baby?" Harvey said taking Millie in his arms and off Willow's breast. He held her close, taking her paci and placing it back in her mouth before walking her out to the living room.

"Just wait here little one, Daddy just needs a minute," he said, turning on some cartoons for Millie and stroking her hair before going back into the bedroom. When he entered, Willow was redressing herself, slowly zipping up her jacket.

"Cute baby we have, Daddy," Willow said her voice full of challenge. Harvey just closed the door quietly behind him, locking it before turning around and backhanding Willow cross the face, causing her to fall to the floor.

"What the fuck are you playing at bitch?" He hissed in a low tone, burning with rage. Willow opened her mouth to speak, but Harvey slapped her again, grabbing her hair and lifting her to her feet before throwing her back onto the bed. He jumped on top of her and pinned her down, sitting on top of her with his thighs on either side of her waist.

"She wasn't complaining; I guess she's not your perfect baby after all," Willow hissed back copping another slap this time on the other side of her face.

"Is this what you wanted? Did you want to be punished? You didn't want me to let you go, so you try and compromise her?" Harvey said, placing his hand on Willow's throat.

"I just thought maybe you'd want both of us," Willow said as Harvey tightened his grip on her neck. He loosened it in disgust, angry at her and angry at himself for thinking that she could have accepted a clean break. Harvey got off her and walked into the bathroom, looking at himself in the mirror.

"It felt nice, you know, to care for someone. To hold her," Willow said, coming in behind him and placing a hand on his back. He flinched, not wanting to feel what he was feeling. If he had been honest with himself, he would have told Willow he never wanted to lose her. That he had loved fucking her ragged, but that he needed a softer woman as his baby girl. She was the temptress men dream about. The slut that never said no, that was always willing and ready that can seduce even the most loyal man until he is balls deep in her cunt. The power-hungry executive with the heels that conditioned everyone to fear her presence. And Harvey knew it, he knew he loved her for her power and dominance, but he also knew that she was never going to the baby he wanted and he was angry at himself for not having realized this sooner.

"I must admit, I was shocked at how motherly you looked," he said, looking in the mirror at Willow's reflection. She smirked.

"I wasn't prepared for that either," she said, showing him a softer side.

"She's straight, how did you get her to be so relaxed with you?" Harvey said, turning around, for the first time looking at the damage he had done to her face. Frowning, he wet the corner of a washcloth and pressed it to her cheek. Willow just narrowed her eyes and took the cloth from him, holding it to her face.

"I would have done the same, don't worry," she said. Harvey watched as she moved to sit down on the edge of the bath.

"I told her that Daddy had gone out and that Mama was going to look after her. She was very confused," Willow said, clearly impressed with herself. Harvey laughed and came to sit next to her.

"And?" He prompted knowing that there was more to the story.

"I said Daddy was silly for not telling her about me and that she should get used to Mama touching her," Willow said, shrugging her shoulders.

"I'm just sexy, what can I say, baby girl loved Mama's big titties," Willow joked rubbing her hands over her breasts and bouncing them in her hands.

"So, you want to play happy families?" He said, passing her the soothing balm for her red face and neck. Willow sat and thought before standing up and walking towards the bedroom door.

"Yeah," she said winking as she unlocked the door and walked down the hallway.

"Where's Mama's good girl?" Willow called out making Harvey jump to his feet and follow her out into the living room. Millie had been watching the cartoons Harvey had left on for her as Willow sat down next to her and wrapped her arm and Millie.

"Such a sweetheart," Willow said as Harvey came to sit on Millie's other side.

"Daddy," Millie said, snuggling into him. Millie wrapped her arms around Harvey's waist, and he felt his heart soften instantly.

"Oh baby girl," he said, picking her up and placing her on his lap. Millie rested her head on his shoulder as he rocked her gently, Willow moving closer to sit next to him. Placing her hand on his crotch, Harvey put Millie to one side and away from Willow's hands.

"Mama, what are you doing?" Millie suddenly said making Willow smirk and look up.

"I'm going to make Daddy happy, baby girl, do you want to watch or not?" Willow said more gently than Harvey had ever heard her speak before. He frowned as he thought about all the times he had tried to get Willow to show a softer side, surprised that it had been his baby girl who had made it happen. Willow suddenly pulled his cock from his pants and began sucking, ripping him out of his daydream and causing him to gasp.

"I guess you're going to watch little one," Willow said, stopping briefly to smile wickedly at Millie. Millie, feeling uncomfortable with the situation, took out her paci suddenly and stood up, as though snapping out of the daze she had been in since arriving at Harvey's house the day before.

"I've got to go," she said, running into his bedroom and locking the door behind her before he had the chance to stop her.

"Millie, open up baby," Harvey said banging on the door. There was desperation in his voice, not wanting to lose her. Millie took off her onesie, diaper, and socks before going to the bathroom and showering. She hadn't heard Harvey take an axe and break through his bedroom door, but as she left the bathroom with just her towel, she saw him standing in the room holding the axe.

"Harvey, please don't," Millie said, instantly scared that he would hurt her. Frowning in confusion before realizing what she was afraid of, Harvey dropped the axe.

"Oh no no Millie, I just used it to break the door down. You're ok; you're safe, Millie. I'm not going to hurt you," he said to Millie who had begun to cry.

"It's just all too much; I can't. Please let me

go home," Millie said softly and looking into her towel. Harvey sat on the edge of his bed and looked down to the floor.

"Yeah I'm sorry, I shouldn't have left this morning, this isn't the way I wanted it to go down," he said, shaking his head.

"You should have just told me about her, I've never been with a woman, but like, I've never called someone Daddy or wore a diaper either, I would have been cool with it if you have just told me," Millie said looking around for her clothes. Harvey had washed and ironed them before he had gone to buy breakfast and got up, remembering where he had got them from.

"Millie, she shouldn't have even been here. We aren't together. I let her stay here when her ex kicked her out, and we had just been fucking for a while. I'm not with her, and in fact, she had been looking for a new place to move into," Harvey said, passing Millie her clothes. Millie just shook her head as she got dressed, trying to process what he was telling her.

"She was just trying to get back at me for telling her that she had to move out, I'm so sorry she has done this to you," Harvey said taking the towel from Millie and placing it in the bathroom.

"Harvey, I just can't," Millie said, placing her hand on his chest before leaving the room. Harvey nodded, understanding that things had gone way too far and stayed in the room, not wanting to make it any harder for Millie to leave.

"Going so soon, baby girl?" Willow said seeing Millie walk towards the door. Millie just looked at her, her broken-heart eyes catching Willow off guard who softened immediately.

"Hey look, I'm sorry," Willow said, standing up and hurrying over to where Millie stood.

"Don't," Millie said as Willow placed both her hands on Millie's shoulders forcing her to face her.

"Millie, Harvey is a great guy, I shouldn't have done that, I'm sorry," Willow said catching the tear that escaped Millie's eyes and pulling her to her chest, embracing her, surprised that the younger woman could make her feel so moved.

"Please, just let me go," Millie said, pushing Willow away gently, breaking the embrace and turning to walk out the front door.

Chapter 6

"Are you going to get out of bed?" Willow asked Harvey who had stayed in bed for the last two days. He thought back to how he had tried to introduce Millie to his world, how hot Willow and her had looked, how he wished he hadn't gone so far with her so quickly. He had sent her nine messages and hadn't got a reply from one of them. He had even gone to the bar that they had met last week. *That's it, it hasn't even been longer than seven days, and I'm already ruined by her, fuck*, he thought throwing a pillow at Willow who was standing in his doorway. He hadn't bothered to fix the hack job he did on the door.

"No," was all he bothered to say. Willow looked at him with pity in her eyes.

"This is pathetic; you do know that, right?" She said viciously. He didn't want to hear it, throwing another pillow in her direction.

"Fuck off," he said, wondering how she had become the one with reason and logic. He knew she was right, which irritated him.

"Why are you still in my house?" He suddenly asked, wondering what it would take for her to leave.

"Oh, you love me being here, who else is going to train all your pretty clients and keep your business alive while you have your tantrum?" Willow smirked, remembering how a blonde with a thick booty licked her pussy when she sat on her face.

"What?" Harvey asked, confused. Willow just rolled her eyes and came to sit next to him on his bed.

"Well, while you have been in here, I've been out there, training and fucking your pretty little clients. Don't worry; they've loved it. I told them I'm your new assistant," Willow said, clearly impressed with herself. Harvey just pulled the blankets over his head and groaned.

"Do you know how long I have worked to

get that all up and running and you are just coming in and fucking with it?" He said, hiding under the blankets. Willow smirked to herself before getting up and walking out of the room.

"Hey, I wasn't finished feeling sorry for myself," Harvey called out to her, deciding that he needed to get up and get to work before she fucked his business into the ground.

Millie had been numb since she left Harvey's home. She had done the usual things, gone to work, exercised at the gym and tried to bring herself down from the whirlwind weekend she had experienced at Harvey's. Everything about her time with him made her head spin. The care that he had taken with her, seeming to know just how far to push and pull her, the way that he was fully present when she was talking to him, and then there was Willow. *She is just a whole other level I'm not even getting into right now*, Millie thought, dismissing the memory of Willow's overwhelmingly seductive presence.

Looking out the window, Millie saw her reflection as the bus drove through a tunnel. Her sad eyes made her own heart, ache at the image of a woman she hardly recognized. Looking away and out into the mass of people all blankly staring back at her. *I wonder if they can see it, see what I've done, see what he did, and see what I let him do. See what she did*, Millie thought blushing as she remembered how it felt to be diapered and given a paci to suck. Quickly turning back to stare out the window, she squeezed her eyes shut as to try and push the memory from her mind and out of her heart. Failing, she dipped her head and let the images of Willow's huge breast and Harvey's kind eyes as he pushed his cock deep inside of her relentlessly, using her until he was satisfied but making her feel safer than she ever had flood her mind.

"Hey, you need to speak with Harvey," Millie heard a voice say behind her. She was buying groceries and had reached up to take a packet of cake mix down from the top shelf, having to stand on her tippy toes to reach. Turning around, Willow was standing behind her, her hands on her hips of her skinny black jeans, her cream heels tapping a toe impatiently. Millie just looked at her. With her beige trench coat and V-neck black sweater, her eyes were more piercing than Millie remembered, seeing Willow's sensual smoky eye and perfect highlight rendering her speechless.

"I don't know what to say to him," Millie softly finally said to which Willow just laughed.

"How about, hey Daddy I miss you come back to me?" Willow said causing Millie to try and hush her as she looked around the store frantically, hoping that no-one had heard Willow who just smirked in amusement.

"Do you miss him?" Willow suddenly asked, wondering if she had missed something.

"Yes, of course," Millie said defensively before realizing what she had said and reflected on her words.

"Well then little girl," Willow teased holding

out her hand to Millie.

"What?" Millie said, wondering what Willow wanted. Willow just rolled her eyes and reached down taking Millie's hand in hers.

"That's no way to speak to Mama," Willow said, enjoying Millie's discomfort.

"You're not my Mama," Millie muttered stubbornly making Willow laugh.

"True, however," Willow said, turning Millie around to look at her, suddenly becoming very serious.

"Harvey does miss you, and if it hadn't been for my, games shall we say, you two would be happily playing house instead of feeling miserable. Millie, he cares about you. I've never seen him so destroyed by a woman before, and I kinda think you haven't had a guy like him before and maybe that's exactly what you need," Willow said speaking candidly, making Millie feel the truth of her words in the pit of her being.

"He's over there sweetie, go and talk to him," Willow almost pleaded. She watched Millie as she slowly turned to see Harvey trying to decide which pasta to buy, reading both labels at the same time. Millie turned back to Willow, who placed her two fingers to Millie's lips when she began to speak.

"Go!" Willow said, practicing her Mama voice on Millie who was taken aback by how commanding Willow sounded.

"Yes Ma'ma," Millie muttered gaining a slap on her ass as she passed Willow who stood by Millie's shopping trolley feeling very impressed with her matchmaking abilities.

"It doesn't matter which one you buy; they are both shit. Get this one instead," Millie said as confidently as she could fake, holding up the most expensive packet of pasta she had quickly found. Harvey looked up, surprised to be seeing Millie standing in front of him.

"Hi," she said softly, tucking her hair behind her ear. Harvey just looked at her like she had answered his most troubling question, shaking his head to try and keep the conversation alive.

"Um, hi," was all that he could manage before he started smiling like a schoolboy.

"You're speaking with me," he gushed, blushing slightly. Millie smiled at her feet, her feelings for Harvey flooding her veins in the strongest pull she had ever felt.

"Yeah well, I couldn't let you buy that rubbish. And also, I was afraid of what Willow would do to me if I didn't talk to you," Millie said, laughing looking up to see Willow walking over to the pair.

"You're welcome. Now off you go, go do some Daddy baby girl activities together and live happily ever after," she said, laughing to herself and placing all Millie's groceries into Harvey's shopping trolley.

"What? Are you going to let her starve?" Willow asked Harvey who was looking at her in a panic.

"Millie, it's ok I don't expect you to," Harvey said, being surprised he was cut off by Millie who just placed her fingers to his lips.

"Shh, Daddy," Millie softly said, taking the pasta from his hands and dropping it into the trolley as well, beaming cheekily up at him.

"I'm glad that worked. My next thought was to hold the photos of you to ransom," Willow said, making both Harvey and Millie spin around and look at her.

"What photos?!" They both asked, Harvey, shaking his head wondering what damage Willow was trying to do next.

"These," Willow said showing Millie a photo of herself, the morning she had woken up with Willow sitting next to her.

"You have to delete them, please Willow," Millie begged in a hushed voice as someone passed them. Willow stared her down, pleasantly surprised when Millie refused to back down.

"Oh baby girl, you've got some steel under that soft shell. Here, look it's gone. Which is a real shame because you looked adorable!" Willow said teasingly.

"Is she out of the house?" Millie asked

Harvey, who laughed at her direct tone.

"Yes, Millie, she is. She left two days after, you know, everything turned to shit," Harvey said, regret in his voice. Millie took his hand and snuggled into his chest, feeling his arms close around her, and she melted into him, feeling at home again.

Chapter 7

Millie met Harvey in a café close to her apartment by the park a week later. She had read up on the frenzied headspace that many new people in the kink community experience and related more to the articles than she wished she had. She had joined forums and groups online that addressed differing elements of the DDlg dynamic and enjoyed learning more about the fluidity of sexuality. She also learned about how some people had MDlg dynamics that were completely no sexual, and she wondered if that was what she wanted to experience with Willow. Quickly deciding that Willow would have fucked her if time had been on her side, Millie laughed to herself and shook her head.

"Hey there sweetie," Harvey said, rushing in. It was raining, and Millie had arrived early, worried that the buses would run late due to the weather. She watched as Harvey took his coat off and ran his fingers through his semi-dry hair, making sure that the style was still maintained.

"You look good, Daddy," Millie said reassuringly in his ear as she passed him and went to get the order she had placed earlier.

"Clever girl," Harvey said when Millie came back and placed his coffee in front of him. Millie smiled and looked into his eyes.

"What are you having?" Harvey asked curiously, peering into her glass. Millie had started drinking green juices for breakfast, and Harvey noticed that she had lost some of her softness. Today though, she was not holding back and had ordered a caramel fudge latte with extra cream and sprinkles.

"It's called the Rocket, I guess because it sends your sugar levels over the moon," Millie said making Harvey laugh.

"This is nice. Thank you for being so open to this and us. I'm truly sorry about how it all started," Harvey said, shaking his head before sipping his black coffee. He took the biscuit that had come with his coffee and scooped up some cream from Millie's drink on the edge.

"Tasty," he said before going back for more. Millie sat back in her chair and looked at Harvey. He met her eyes and kept her gaze, staying in that moment in time with her, letting the rest of the world fade away. Millie couldn't remember a time when everything had fallen so utterly into place. The sun broke through the clouds, beaming into the café and onto their faces, making both of them squint but continue to look at each other.

"Let's do this," Millie said, standing up and holding out her hand to Harvey.

"Where are we going?" Harvey asked, enjoying following Millie out of the café, flicking up his coat with one hand.

"I've seen your place, but you haven't seen mine," Millie said hailing a taxi impressing Harvey with her wolf whistle.

"Yeah, I've got some tricks, Daddy," Millie said cheekily winking at him. Harvey grinned back at her but didn't respond; he was just enjoying falling into her world.

The taxi took them 15 blocks away from the city and to the edge of a nature reserve and into the driveway of a small white apartment building with a white picket fence, and red rose bushes in full bloom out the front.

"Wow, this is lovely baby," Harvey said, paying the taxi driver catching Millie off guard.

"Oh, I hope that was ok, I just," Harvey said, not wanting to push Millie too far again.

"No it's nice, I just wasn't expecting it. I like that you take care of things like that, Daddy," Millie said, opening her gate and being greeted by a large black cat.

"I hope you're not allergic, Daddy," Millie said, scratching the cat behind the ears before walking up to the door.

"She's not mine, she's sort of like the neighborhoods, that's why she's so fat," Millie laughed as the cat walked into her apartment as though she owned it.

"That's funny. No, I'm not allergic to anything," Harvey said, looking around Millie's homely country style home.

"You have exquisite taste," Harvey said, sitting down on her Chesterfield couch and spreading his arms out along the back of the leather.

"I'm glad you like it," Millie said, turning the heating on.

"Do you want a drink or anything?" Millie asked as Harvey jumped up and walked into her kitchen behind her. He placed his hands on her hips and pressed play on the playlist he had made for her, swaying her hips in time with his, pressing into her.

"Daddy," Millie said, feeling her body grow warm in anticipation. Harvey twirled her before bringing her close to him again.

"Yes?" He playfully asked, cupping her breasts in his hands over her soft, fluffy light yellow sweater.

"These look so good. Let Daddy have a little

look," Harvey said, lifting the sweater slightly and seeing that Millie's bra matched. He reached roughly into her bra and pulled her tits out, making them rest over her bra, flicking her nipples until he had made them so sensitive that Millie pulled away from him. Laughing he reached around and unhooked her bra and pulled the straps down, throwing her bra on the floor and rubbing her tits over her sweater he had pulled back down.

"Daddy doesn't want you wearing a bra when it's just you and I in either of our houses. Is that ok princess?" Harvey asked Millie.

"Yes, Daddy," Millie replied as Harvey sat down at her kitchen table and pulled her onto his lap. He took his time groping her, having missed playing with her. Millie just rested her head back on his shoulder and stuck out her chest, giving him full access to what he desired. It didn't surprise her that she felt him growing under her skirt sooner rather than later, feeling him shift her on his lap, taking his predatory hands away only to reach under her skirt and spread her ass cheeks either side of his cock.

"You'll feel it sticking into your pussy soon little girl, will you let Daddy fuck today?" Harvey whispered in Millie's ear as he went back to using his hands on her tits, enjoying his intentional degrading. He liked that he felt like a dirty older man preying on his young victim, Millie's ever eager submission to him driving him wild.

"Yes, Daddy," Millie gasped as she did feel Harvey's huge cock tilt up and press into her slit. He grunted as he lifted her off his lap enough to force her to take his cock sliding back and forth along her already wet slit.

"I'm happy you didn't wear any panties like Daddy told you. You're a good girl, aren't you Millie?" Harvey said, pulling at her skirt.

"Take it off," he instructed. Millie stood up and began swinging her hips in time with the music, twirling on the spot and slowly unzipping the back of her skirt in front of Harvey. She spread her thighs and straddled his leg as she undid the skirt entirely and let it drop on the floor, her naked pussy beginning to grind on his thigh in time to the music. Harvey leaned back and watched as her ass bounced and jiggled on him, slapping her thighs and taking the small butt plug from his pocket.

"Bend forward," he commanded, slapping her ass one final time. He spat on the plug and began pushing it into Millie's ass, making her gasp and moan.

"Keep it in," Harvey said as Millie reached back around her ass and spread her cheeks to adjust the plug inside her comfortably.

"Daddy's, precious little princess," Harvey said, standing up, making Millie do the same.

"Show Daddy where we are playing, baby girl," he said, gripping Millie on the back of her neck and picking up his bag as she led him to her bedroom.

He threw her onto her bed and took in the room. It had soft furnishings, a fireplace, and thick pink fur rug on the floor. Harvey took out three black satin ties and draped them over Millie's tummy.

"Take your sweater off, little one," he instructed, lighting a fire before turning around to see that Millie had followed his instruction.

"Good," he said, looking at her unmarked skin. Harvey took one of the ties and began tying up Millie's tits, starting on the left side, he grabbed at her and pulled her tit out towards him.

"Ripe and ready to be taken aren't you," he said enjoying how Millie's breast became hard, her nipple poking out as he tied one and then the other.

"Look at you," he said, standing back and looking at his handy work. He had tied Millie so that her wrists were bound behind her back and her tits were forced out from her chest, on display for his enjoyment. Touching her, he smirked as she shuddered when he ran his fingernails over the tops of her tits, the skin being pulled tight.

"I'm going to enjoy those," Harvey said as he brought both his hands down to slap them, making Millie scream.

"Hmm, you might be a bit too loud, let

Daddy fix that," Harvey said looking into his bag and pulling out a dildo gag like the one Millie had shown him a photo of.

"Does this look familiar? Daddy knows how you like to suck cock; now you can while I play with you," he said, pushing the soft object into her mouth and down her throat.

"Now, where was I, oh yes," Harvey said, picking Millie up and placing her on her knees on her pink rug. He sat on the edge of the bed and slowly took off his shoes, followed by his belt, jeans, and briefs.

"Have you missed Teddy, baby girl? He has missed you," Harvey said, reaching forward and pulling Millie close to him as he began to rub his cock over her big tits in their firm restraints. Millie felt his touch more intensely and moaned as she closed her eyes and sucked on the dildo strapped to her mouth.

"Yeah, Daddy's dirty girl," Harvey said as he flicked her nipples with his pre-cumming cock, making her nipples wet and sticky. He grabbed two handfuls of Millie's bound breasts and pulled her closer again as he slid his cock between her helpless tits.

"Daddy is going to cover you in cum," Harvey said as he began fucking Millie's tits roughly, reaching under the tie and holding it firmly in one hand as he slid up and down her deep crease, her nipples shaking as he thrust hard and came over the tops of her tits.

"Oh yeah, Daddy gave you those porn star titties. You gonna be my little porn star tonight, baby girl," Harvey said as he pushed her onto her back and kneed over her, fucking her tits again. This time he knew where he wanted to cum and took the gag from Millie's mouth, covering her mouth with his hand, not interested in hearing her moans. He felt his balls get full and his cock surge as he groped one of Millie's tits as he fucked her helpless body before taking his hand away and pushing his cock down her throat, cumming in her as she gagged and choked on his monster.

"Yeah, that's what I expect from my baby

girl, that you take what Daddy gives you without complaining," Harvey said picking her up and placing her on his lap and down on his cock. Millie gasped as she was unexpectedly filled, Harvey cumming again inside her. He bounced her on his lap, watching as her bound tits bounced and jiggled, his cum dripping from her nipples. Millie felt him more intensely with the plug in her ass and knew that she was close to her limit. Harvey could feel it too as she became quiet.

"Daddy's good girl," he said cumming one last time before quickly untying her, her tits feeling blood flow back into them and her wrists getting pins and needles as he rubbed them lovingly.

"I loved that, Daddy," Millie said, surprised that she had been the one to suggest most of the scene, the previous week.

Chapter 8

Harvey knew what he wanted as he watched Millie sleep in her bed. This time after their night together, he hadn't left. Instead, he had made a coffee, gone back to bed and watched Millie as she curled up in the blankets. She had rolled into his lap and he re-positioned his legs so that she was laying between them, her mouth close to his cock. Drinking his coffee as he stroked Millie's hair, he pressed his cock covered sweat pants to her lips, smirking as she pouted her lips in a kiss. Feeling it wiggle with excitement, he reached into his pants and took it out, jerking his balls in one hand and holding Millie's head down on his lap as he rubbed his hardening cock against her soft cheek. Pressing the tip down as it formed its hard shaft, Harvey rubbed the tip over her lips, groaning in anticipation as her lips were forced open around the top.

"Suck," Harvey whispered lovingly, pulling on his sack as Millie opened her mouth and he pushed into her, past her teeth to the soft stop he wanted and slowly pulled back out.

"Good girl," he said, taking her face in both his hands as he face fucked her awake. He knew he'd have to hold her down as her eyes opened and she startled, trying to pull away from him, he just pushed into her further, forcing her throat open.

"Take it," Harvey roughly growled, holding her face to his balls, his cock throbbing down her neck as he squirted into her. Millie's eyes watered with the sensation and he held the back of her head to him as his other hand reached under the blankets to toy with her cunt.

"Don't you dare try and take it out, you'll take Daddy when and how I want, remember, princess?" Harvey warned, reminding Millie of the commitment she had made to him. She just nodded as the dick she had in her mouth prevented her from being able to speak.

"Yeah, I bet you do," Harvey said as he went back to thrusting his rod down her throat. Taking his cock out suddenly, Millie gasped for air as he turned her over and ripped the bed sheets back. He took her by her hips, picked her up, and pushed her against a wall, fucking her in the air.

"I'm going to carry you around the house all day with Teddy buried deep inside of you. You're going to be locked into Daddy, unable to escape every pump of my cock I want to fill you with," Harvey whispered as Millie wrapped her arms around his head and tried to lift off him as her orgasm ravaged her. Harvey just laughed as he stuck his thumb in her ass suddenly, making her gasp and try to wiggle away from him.

"What did Daddy just say?" He said, holding Millie slightly away from him and humping her roughly, wanting to empty his load in her as he anchored her to him with his thumb starting to wiggle inside her making her moaning as she was taken with primal force.

"Yeah, that's it, cum for Daddy, little girl,"

Harvey said, as Millie panted. He had taken her around to the kitchen as he placed her on her back on the counter and watched as his cock filled her, pushing her tummy out with each pump, cream dripping down her thighs.

"Daddy's not finished yet," Harvey said, picking her back up and keeping his cock pounding her as he walked to the living room and roughly threw her down on the couch. Grabbing her ankles, he held her legs open as he pulled her cunt to him, sliding his cock in balls deep, again before leaning over her and driving his massive shaft into her, drilling her hard.

"Turn around," he said, pulling out of her and turning her around. He slapped her bubble butt, taking two hand-fills and shaking it.

"Shake your ass for Daddy," Harvey instructed as Millie got to her knees and twerked for him as he placed the tip of his wet cock into her ass, making her groan.

"I didn't say stop," he said, grabbing her ponytail and roughly pulling her head back to look at him. He slapped her ass repeatedly; he stuffed her ass with his cock as she twerked for him. Making her scream as she was stretched, Harvey continued to spank her ass red, enjoying the whimpers she began to gasp.

"You like this don't you, this is what you need," Harvey said, putting two fingers in Millie's mouth, fish hooking her as he slowly fucked her ass.

"Yes, Daddy," Millie said around the big fingers filling her mouth.

"Oh I just want to stuff all your holes," Harvey said, pumping her ass harder while his free hand stopped spanking her and reached under her and into her used cunt.

"I wonder if Daddy can fist you, little girl," Harvey said quickly slipping three fingers inside Millie. He knew he didn't have long to play when she began to resist him, her pussy clenching and her head trying to shake his fingers from her mouth. Forcefully, he stuffed another finger inside of her as she came hard, falling limp on the couch as he finished his onslaught, fucking her long enough to remind her that he was in charge, but softly enough for her to know that he cared for her. Pulling out of her ass, cunt, and mouth all at once, Millie felt empty as Harvey dumped his load onto her tits, fucking them as he held them together in his big hands. He was sliding his still throbbing cock up and down the soft tunnel he had made.

"Yeah, you're just for Daddy aren't you," Harvey said as he came again, cum squirting up and around her neck, dribbling back down onto the tops of her tits. Standing up and looking down on his baby girl, Harvey smiled at how she had taken him. Her holes are dripping cum onto herself, her hair a mess, her ass red, her tits covered in his cream.

"Pretty girl," Harvey said, picking her up gently, holding her tenderly in his arms.

"Have I fucked you good, little girl," Harvey said, walking her to the bath.

"But now I want more," he added, making

Millie's eyes go wide.

"I don't think I can take anymore, Daddy," Millie said, worried at what Harvey wanted with her body now. Harvey just laughed as he ran the bath water for Millie.

"No, little one, Daddy wants his baby girl back. Not the little slut I just used like I'd paid for her," Harvey said, lowering Millie into the warm water. He left the bathroom, returning with bubble bath and bath ducks.

"Do you like duckies little one?" He asked, watching as Millie entered her little space.

"Yeah, Daddy," she excitedly said, clapping her hands. Harvey washed her body clean as Millie played with the toys before taking her out and drying her off.

"Daddy, I hurt here," Millie said, referring to her ass. Harvey just nodded and took her hand as he led her to the bedroom. He picked the blankets he had thrown on the floor and lay Millie down on top as he took out a puffy white diaper.

"I bet it does, you were such a good girl for

Daddy, let me have a look," Harvey said opening a tub of thick, soothing balm and gently rubbing it over Millie's ass-hole.

"It might hurt for a little while, but Daddy will keep looking after it, ok?" Harvey asked Millie who could only nod. He had given her a pink paci, happy that Millie was such an obedient girl. He sprinkled the powder over her pussy, rubbing it in so she wouldn't chaff and tighten the tabs around her waist.

"Daddy wants to go out for brunch today, so, you'll have to wear some big girl clothes, but you'll keep your diapy on," Harvey said, slapping Millie's thighs as she tried to speak.

"I didn't ask what you wanted, it doesn't matter, you are Daddy's little girl, and you'll do as you're told," Harvey said firmly. He went to Millie's cupboard and looked through her clothes. Selecting a pair of black stockings, a black pinafore dress and a white T-shirt he walked back over to were Millie was rolling around on the bed, enjoying the feeling of the thick padding pushing her thighs open, exposing her to Harvey who rubbed her lustfully.

"Such a pretty girl," He said, and she knew that he wanted to fuck her again. He carefully rolled the stockings over her toes and up her calves, stopping and standing back, enjoying how she looked, her thighs being forced to close around the thick padding he knew would be rubbing on her clit and pussy.

"Do you like your diapy, baby girl?" Harvey asked, going back to her cupboard and taking out a light pink bra.

"It'll match your paci, everyone will think you are so cute," Harvey said stroking her face with his index finger before sitting her up, holding her as her abs ached and she winced in pain.

"Shh, Daddy's got you," Harvey said filling the cups of her bra with her juicy tits, making them bounce as he pulled on the straps, delighting his cock which moved in desire. Going back, Harvey continued to roll the stockings up Millie's thighs and over her thick diaper, making it squish into her as he secured the stockings over it. He took her T-shirt and carefully pulled it over her head and ran his hands over her tits as he covered them with the tight shirt.

"Crawl to Daddy," he instructed, sitting back and watching his baby girl wiggle her puffy diapered bottom as she moved to him. Picking her up under her arms, Harvey stood her up and finished her look by zipping up her pinafore dress at the back and helping her slip into her ballet flats.

"How do you want your hair, little one?" Harvey asked, taking out the paci Millie didn't want to let go.

"Like this, Daddy," Millie said, running into the bathroom, coming back and taking his hand when he didn't follow her, Millie walked back into the bathroom and pushed him onto the edge of the bath, making him sit down. Harvey liked how excited Millie was, as she climbed up onto his lap before she started to do her hair in a messy pony-tail.

"That's what you like?" Harvey asked Millie who had started to give his face little kisses.

"Yes, Daddy," Millie said excitedly. He had to admit; it did suit her. Her sparkling blue eyes smiled as he picked her up and carried her back into the bedroom.

"What should Daddy wear today?" Harvey asked Millie despite having no intention of actually letting her have a say in his outfit.

"Something pretty," Millie giggled making Harvey laugh despite himself. He took out his tan, Italian leather boots, thick denim, dark navy jeans, and a tight white T-shirt.

"Look, baby girl, Daddy is going to match with you," Harvey said, referring to their shirts. Next, he took his designer tan leather jacket and put it on, playfully flexing for Millie who just laughed.

"Daddy, you're so silly," she laughed as Harvey opened his arms wide and scooped Millie up in huge bear hug.

"I love you, Millie," Harvey said before

realizing the words had escaped. Millie looked up at him, touching his face, her eyes melting his heart and her cheeky smile, making him beam.

"I love you too Harvey," Millie said, taking the moment he had given them. Staying in that space, he kissed her passionately using his tongue to part her lips, wanting to devour her. Millie, wanting to go back to her little space, playfully pushed him off her.

"Daddy!" She squealed, making Harvey laugh and bend his head.

"What can I say, princess, you're just so tempting," he said, taking her hand deciding that it was time to go before he ravaged her again, unsure of how her body would cope.

Chapter 9

"I thought you said we were going to brunch, Daddy?" Millie asked as Harvey who was happily singing along to a country song that played on the radio. Millie looked out the window and saw the tree-lined gravel track they were driving along. Finishing his song, Harvey turned the radio down and looked at Millie. Placing a hand up her skirt, he carelessly groped her diapered pussy, groaning in frustration as he remembered how she took him so obediently.

"We are going for brunch. Brunch with a friend of Daddy's. He lives just up here," Harvey said, lifting the skirt of her pinafore and taking her hands to hold it back for him.

"Yeah, good girl," Harvey said sincerely as he stroked and cupped her roughly. Driving into a clearing, Millie saw the shed looking building and was surprised when she saw the ogre looking man walk from the front.

"He's your friend?" Millie said shocked that Harvey would know someone so different to him. The man was roughly the same build, but instead of muscle, he just had mass. His head was shaved, and he had tattoos on both his hands. He wore a baggy black T-shirt and loose fitting blue washed jeans and big chunky work boots.

"Kept your skirt up," Harvey said, narrowing his eyes on Millie as she began to cover herself. Surprised, Millie lifted her skirt again just as the man appeared at the window and looked straight onto her pussy. He opened Millie's door and blocked her way, smiling down at her. *At least he has nice teeth and smells good*, Millie thought realising that he couldn't be poor by how white and polished his teeth were and the expensive smell of his cologne.

"Well well, what do we have here," the man teased bopping Millie on the tip of her nose before looking over at Harvey.

"Hey man," Harvey said, getting out the car

and coming around to shake his hand.

"This is Millie; she's a cutie, isn't she?" Harvey said, taking Millie from the car and holding her in his arms. Millie buried her face into Harvey's chest and peeped out at the man.

"Millie, this is Uncle Ben, he is a friend of Daddy," Harvey said, patting her bottom as he walked her inside.

"She's a shy little one," Ben said, brushing her cheek with his thumb.

"Bring her over here, I've got some new toys," Ben said to Harvey as they entered his house. Millie's tummy grumbled, making both the robust men laugh.

"Maybe we fill her up first," Ben said, walking in the opposite direction. Millie hoped he meant brunch, whenever Harvey spoke like that he fucked her to exhaustion and Millie wasn't sure how she felt with the idea of letting this big ogre with his big sausage fingers plow her.

"There you go," Harvey said, placing Millie down in an adult-sized high-chair and securing her in place with a belt around her waist and between her thighs. Millie looked shocked as Harvey left her to go into the fridge and begin to help Ben prepare brunch.

"There's a bottle warmer over there, I moved it," Ben said plainly as Harvey took a bottle of cold milk from the fridge.

"You'll have a bottle today little girl; Mama isn't here to push her big nipple into your mouth. Although, I heard she started to lactate so you might be lucky if you see her again," Harvey laughed. Ben looked at him with a curious expression.

"Willow," was all Harvey had to say before Ben was laughing.

"Yeah I heard she's come over to our side in a big way," Ben said, placing strips of bacon in a saucepan and frying eggs in another one.

"Yeah, well. Imagine my surprise when I come home and there she is, with my little angel's lips pressed to her huge jugs," Harvey said. Millie hadn't heard him speak like that before and she smirked as she remembered how much she had enjoyed it.

"Here sweetheart," Ben said offering Millie a small piece of bacon he blew on to cool down.

"Thank you, Uncle Ben," Millie said politely. Ben smirked.

"Cute, kid," Ben said, patting her on the head. Harvey beamed at her, and she liked that she made him happy.

"Open wide, little one," he said coming over with the bottle he had been warming. Millie took the bottle in both her hands and began drinking.

"She's a good girl," Harvey said, kissing her cheek and going back into the kitchen to sit at the large stone table where Ben had set up their meal. He sat down to a large wooden plate full of bacon, eggs, tomato, and home-made bread that was still warm. Millie couldn't hear them talking and finishing her bottle, she grew bored and wanted to explore. Trying to open the locked belt holding her down, she fiddled with it, getting caught by Ben who had walked back over to her.

"Oh, you want to get down? Say the magic words little girl," Ben said, reaching out to place his big hands on the lock, pushing into her diaper as he waited.

"Please, Uncle Ben," Millie said, hoping that she had got it right. Ben just laughed and shook his head.

"No, how about, I want your cock, Uncle Ben," he said, Millie's mouth gaped open.

"Oh, do you want my cock in your mouth, are you opening it for me?" Ben teased, making Millie shut her mouth quickly. Ben just laughed as he unlocked her harness and took her down. He took his time picking her up, deciding that he wanted her facing him as he carried her. Placing one hand on her back, he pushed her tits into his broad chest as his other hand reached around Millie's ass and between her thighs, pressing his hand into her diaper and against her pussy.

"Safe and sound. I could just slip my cock into you in this position. You'd better stop moving or I might just," Ben said, dropping Millie slightly and pushing the hardening bulge in his pants against her diaper covered pussy.

"Do you feel that pretty baby, that's a big toy for you to play with," Ben teased, rubbing Millie's diaper over his groin. Millie wiggled in his arms, wanting to get down as he carried her back into the room where Harvey was finishing his coffee.

"She's a little squirmer, Daddy," Ben said, placing Millie on Harvey's lap, watching as she settled straight away.

"Did she use the magic words?" Harvey asked suddenly cuffing Millie's wrists behind her back and turning her around to face Ben. Ben pushed his hips forward, enjoying how close Millie's lips were to the thick prick he wasn't even trying to hide.

"You won't need your hands for a while," Harvey said as Millie tried to struggle free. Ben just sat back down and enjoyed watching Millie's tits bounce and shake as Harvey began to bounce her on his lap.

"You lucky bastard," Ben playfully said reaching forward and slapping Millie's tits a few times predatorily. He stood up and went to the kitchen, slicing a piece of bread and drizzling honey over the top. Coming back, Harvey placed one arm around her waist and the other on the front of her chest, holding her jaw open.

"Don't fight Daddy," Harvey said, waiting until Millie stopped moving on his lap. He liked how her resistance hardened his cock, knowing that it would be resting inside her shortly. Millie ate the bread Ben fed her, breaking off small pieces and waiting for her first to swallow before he fed her the next mouthful. Beginning to feel full, Millie shook her head to the last three bit of the large piece of bread.

"Time for a little rest pretty baby," Ben said gesturing for Harvey to follow him down to the other side of the property. Millie could feel her pussy getting wet at the game they were playing, knowing that at some point, she would have two cocks dominating her bound body.

"Put her in here," Ben said, opening the door to a nursery. Millie's eyes grew wide seeing the setup. There was a large adult sized crib with soft sheets printed with fairies. A toy-box overflowing with stuffies was in the corner, and a changing table that was stocked with diapers, creams and lotions, and a box of pacifiers was placed against the wall. Millie saw that it had restraints like the high-chair had and as Harvey carried her to the crib, she giggled in delight.

"Thank you, Daddy," Millie whispered before Harvey placed a blue paci in her mouth. He smiled lovingly as he took her wrists and gently secured the locks around the silk ties.

"I can't have you escaping can I, baby girl?" Harvey said. Millie just shook her head before watching Harvey leave the room. He shut the door behind him, and Millie was surprised at how dark the room was as she closed her eyes and drifted off to sleep.

Waking up, Millie was still in darkness, but she

knew that someone else was in the room with her.

"I was wondering when you'd wake up, little girl," she heard coming from behind the crib. She knew it was Ben. She hoped that Harvey knew he was in here and that it wasn't going to be another Willow incident.

"Daddy," Millie said, pushing her paci out with her tongue.

"No, Daddy's in the living room, I'm just coming in here to get you," Ben said, opening the black-out curtains to let the moonlight stream in.

"Night-time?" Millie asked, making Ben laugh.

"Yeah, little girl, night-time. You had a big sleep; we didn't you'd be out for so long," Ben said, unlocking her wrists and picking up her paci before wrapping her in a blanket and picking her up. This time Millie didn't fight his touch. He held her with one arm between her thighs, pushing her diaper into her pussy and let her legs dangle as his other arm held her around her waist and supported her head.

"Look at what sleepy girl I found," Ben said, carrying Millie into the living room, Harvey was indeed sitting in. He had been drinking, Millie could tell by the shared bottle of whiskey on the wooden table between the high-backed chairs they had been sitting in.

"There's my little girl. Put her on the floor; she can play down there while we finish this," Harvey said, pouring Ben another drink before filling his glass. A fire roared in the considerable stone fire-place, and Millie began to feel hot in her stockings as the warmth from the fire filled the air.

"Daddy, I'm hot," Millie said, crawling over to him and resting her head on his lap.

"Then let me take this off," Harvey said, taking her pinafore and stockings off leaving her in her exposed diaper and T-shirt. Ben and Harvey watched her as she played in front of them, making the stuffies that Ben had placed on the floor talk to each other and bending forward to reach the blocks that were out of reach for her stuffie castle.

"Baby, time to go home, today lasted a lot longer than I had planned," Harvey said, making Ben laugh. Millie just shook her head no, making Harvey raise an eyebrow.

"Oh, you've never said no to me before, little girl," he said, standing up and stretching. He knew he was tipsy; he could tell by how powerful he felt.

"I don't wanna go, Daddy," Millie said, continuing to play her game.

"If you don't get up, I'm going to punish you right here in front of Uncle Ben, is that what you want?" Harvey said, walking over to Millie's tower and kicking it over.

"Daddy!" Millie exclaimed, her eyes sparkling with mischief.

"Sounds like she needs a spank," Ben said, standing up and coming to stand over the top of her next to Harvey. Harvey slowly took off his belt, and Millie just turned around and wiggled her puffy bottom in his face, bending down so her face was on the floor and her ass was high in the air.

"Oh, she's asking for it," Ben laughed, slapping his friend on the back and giving him a knowing look. Harvey just nodded at him, causing Ben to smile and begin to take off his belt. Harvey struck her first, making her gasp as he brought his belt down on her padded ass.

"What? You didn't think Daddy was joking when I said that you'd be punished, did you?" Harvey said, watching as Ben belted her next. Millie just gasped as the air was belted from her lungs time after time as Harvey and Ben took it in turns to strike her. Rolling her onto her back, Harvey looked into Millie's eyes to gauge where she was at, happy when he saw her bit her bottom lip and smirk up at him.

"Get on your knees," Harvey roughly said, grabbing her hair and pulling her into position. He sat back down in his chair and watched as Millie placed her hands behind her head like he had trained her to and waited for his next instruction.

"Open your mouth," he said, watching Ben kick off his shoes and pull his cock out. He was hairier than Harvey, liking how his caveman body looked against the women he fucked. Pulling on his dick as he eyed Millie's obedient and vulnerable position, Ben moved into her line of sight, making Millie gasp as she saw his protruding cock pushing through his fist.

"Yeah, exactly," Ben said as he pushed his cock into Millie's mouth until her face was pressed against his dense black fur, burying her nose in his thick patch of black pubic hair.

"Why you fighting?" Ben said, holding her mouth firmly onto him as he felt his cock jerk in excitement in her mouth. Pulling out slowly, he liked the long string of saliva that connected his cock to her mouth before thrusting back into her making it spurt over her face, wetting his furry balls as he forced her to gobble his cock.

"She's a good girl," Ben said, pulling back out, slapping his cock against Millie's face, pushing the tip into her cheek. Harvey had come to sit behind her, taking off her diaper as Ben turkey slapped her until her face was covered with spit and pre-cum.

"You won't need that anymore," Harvey laughed, feeling how heavy Millie had made her diaper. He took a wet wipe and wiped her clean, happy she was such a good girl for wetting her diaper. He walked over to the bin and threw the used diaper and wipes in before coming back to see that Ben was still busy filling her mouth.

"Suck my balls baby," Ben said, jerking his cock as he lowered his hairy, soft sack into her mouth.

"I said take it," Ben growled, slapping Millie's face as she struggled to fit him in her mouth. She sucked deeply, feeling him grab the back of her head and grind himself further down her throat.

"Yeah, there it is. Good girl," Ben said spilling cum from his big mushroomed tip cock onto his hand. Harvey came back behind her and spat on his hand before roughly rubbing it over her pussy.

"Here's, Daddy," he said, shoving his pulsing

cock into Millie's cunt without warning making her scream around Ben's balls, making them vibrate just exciting him more.

"Oh, dude, make her scream again," Ben said, pumping his cock faster and closing his eyes. Harvey just laughed and sucked a butt plug before stuffing her ass. Ben reached down and grabbed at Millie's tits as she screamed again, her throat vibrating against Ben's balls as he came.

"Get her up here," Harvey said, holding her thighs open and lifting her as he stood. Pulling his balls from Millie's mouth, she was surprised they had filled as their size had grown, filling out and looking like a big furry marshmallow. Harvey carried her to the chair he had been previously sitting in and sat her down on his lap, her face towards him resting on his chest.

"Watch this. Bounce for Daddy," Harvey said as Millie immediately began twerking on his lap, her ass wobbling hard, shaking down on his lap as she fucked herself. Ben came behind her and slowly took out the toy that had stretched her ass.

Slowly taking it from her, he liked that her ass gaped, looking ready to be filled again.

"Do you think she can take this monster?" Ben said, rubbing his big mushroom tip against her asshole.

"Yeah, stick it in dude, enjoy her," Harvey said, reaching around and spreading Millie's asshole further. Ben smirked as he stuffed the tip in, feeling Millie, try and close herself.

"Your Daddy said I could have you baby girl, and that's what I'm going to do, I'm going to empty all the cream you just filled my balls within this ass," Ben said grabbing Millie's hair in his fist as his other hand held her down by her shoulder as he speared her ass until he was balls deep inside her just as Harvey thrust into her filling her pussy, both men cumming in her at the same time. Millie squealed as they began fucking her again, their cum spilling from her holes as she was taken by the two large men, being entirely overpowered by their embrace.

"Where do you think you are going?"

Harvey said as Millie wriggled on his lap.

"I told you that you'd be punished didn't I sweetheart," he added, picking her up and pulling his cock from her, making her squirt all over the floor. Ben laughed as his cock made a popping sound as his tip pulled from her ass. Harvey put her down in the cummy mess they had made as Millie's holes oozed cum on the cold, slate floor Harvey had laid her on.

"I don't think there's much use continuing, she's all used up for tonight," he said walking to the kitchen and taking out two beers and opening them on the side of the bench before stepping back, his still erect cock swinging as he walked.

"Cheers," Ben said toasting as he stood on one side of Millie and Harvey standing on the other side.

"Knock knock mother fuckers, I got your text," Millie heard Willow announce as she walked into the room, stopping when she saw Millie laying on the floor.

"What did you do to my little one!?" Willow

exclaimed making Millie burst into tears. She had been happy so far, but something about Willow just made her feel so nervous and more uncomfortable than getting fucked as she had just been fuck did.

"Look, you made her cry," Harvey teased, pouring some of his beer over Millie's face.

"Oh baby girl, come to Mama," Willow said, pushing Harvey away who just laugh before sighing in contented bliss and falling back into his chair.

"Say bye bye to Millie, Teddy," Harvey mocked, shaking his cock at Millie as Willow bent down and took her hand, walking her out of the room.

"She's great, hey? Such a slut," Harvey said, finishing his beer in one chug.

"Yeah dude, and you said she is an accounted? It's always the quiet ones, isn't it?" Ben said, remembering how good it had felt to use Millie.

"Why did you text Willow?" Ben asked,

making Harvey laugh.

"That's my little psychological treat for her. She tries to tell me she's straight, but Willow got her good," Harvey said impressed with himself.

Willow had taken Millie to Ben's shower and washed her clean, making sure to soap her gently. The markings from Harvey and Ben's belts visible despite Millie having had her diaper to protect her ass.

"You must have been such a bad girl to be punished like this little one," Willow said, taking Millie's hand and leading her out of the bath.

"I just said no to Daddy," Millie said, her little voice escaping as she fell back into her small headspace, with Willow being so gentle and loving with her.

"Well, that'll do it," Willow laughed before kissing Millie's cheek.

"But it's ok because Mama is here now and you're always safe with Mama, aren't you?" Willow said. She liked that Millie was so inexperienced with women and just blushed and fought herself over wanting what was happening to her.

"Say it little one," Willow said, catching Millie off guard, not understanding what Willow wanted.

"Say, you are safe with Mama," Willow said, helping Millie understand. Millie burned red and bit her bottom lip, squirming nervously in Willow's hands, and she held the towel still and looked expectantly into Millie's eyes.

"I'm safe with Mama," Millie almost whispered, looking down but not getting further than Willow's big sweater covered tits.

"Soon, little girl," Willow said, catching Millie staring. Millie looked up ready to try and say she wasn't looking, but Willow just raised her eyebrow, and Millie stopped.

"Don't even try to pretend you don't want them. Mama even has a special treat for you," Willow said making Millie remember that Harvey had said Willow had milk now.

"But first, let's get you dressed and all ready

for bed. You've had a big day," Willow said, taking Millie into the nursery and laying her on the changing table. Willow selected a purple diaper and added extra padding, knowing Millie's pussy would be leaking her captures cum for hours to come. Patting Millie as she fastened the sticky tabs down firmly securing the diaper in place.

"Are you going to be Mama's little bunny tonight, sweetheart?" Willow asked, taking out a white fluffy bunny onesie and dressing Millie before she had responded.

"Why am I asking? You'll do everything Mama wants because if you think they punished you, oh little lady, you've never felt Mama's wrath," Willow said putting a white paci in Millie's mouth before helping her down and pushing her to the floor.

"Crawl to Mama, little one," Willow said, walking over to the big rocking chair in the opposite corner and sitting down. She placed Millie on her la, and Millie knew what was going to come next.

"Is this what you want little one?" Willow whispered as she lifted her sweater off her head and pulled out her breast from its cup.

"I'm not really," Millie began to say making Willow rolled her eyes.

"Yeah, I know you're not really into girls, blah blah blah, shut up, baby and suck Mama's milky tits like a good girl," Willow said placing her nipple in Millie's mouth and squeezing her tits making her milk squirt into Millie's mouth.

"Yummy isn't it, little one?" Willow asked, already knowing the answer, watching Millie close her eyes and melt into her arms as she nursed. Millie made soft slurping noises making Willow smile and stroke her cheek as she nursed Millie, her limp body soft and warm in her arms.

"I was wondering how long it would take for you to appear," Willow said seeing Harvey walk into the nursery. He had showered and was wearing comfortable house clothes as he came and stood by Willow's side, bending down to kiss her on the cheek.

"Thanks," he said, referring to the gentle aftercare she was giving Millie.

"How could I say no to this little one?" Willow said making Millie open her eyes.

"Daddy!" She exclaimed happily before going back to suckling on Willow's massive tits as she looked up at him.

"Hey there little one, is Mama looking after you?" Harvey said going over to taking a blanket from the crib and wrapping it over Willow's shoulders.

"Thank you, Daddy," Willow sensually teased.

"I still think we should play happy families, look how much little Millie needs a Mama," Willow said stroking Millie's hair out of her face while rocking her in her arms.

"And look at how much Teddy needs to be kept entertained. Our little girl can't do that job all by herself, we both know that" Willow said grabbing Harvey's cock, feeling it harden immediately as she stroked him.

"I'll think about it," he said in a hoarse throat making Millie laugh.

"What are you laughing at hey," Harvey said, kissing her forehead.

"You, Daddy. Why are you pretending you don't love Mama," Millie asked around Willow's nipple, milk spilling from her mouth and down her cheek.

"Yeah, Daddy, why do you pretend you don't love me?" Willow asked more serious than Harvey was prepared for. He walked over to the changing table and took a wet-wipe before passing it to Willow and deeply thinking about the proposal.

"What would that even look like?" He asked coming to sit in front of Willow on the floor, crossing his legs and beginning to rub her feet.

"I could get used to this," Willow said, bouncing Millie gently as Harvey massaged her heels.

"I guess our little one would go to work Monday-Friday, see her friends on the weekend.

Be our baby every night, and when you've destroyed her, Mama can come and look after her before she goes and finishes you off. I would move my stuff back into your house; Millie would move in too. You'd still work like you do, so would I, we could go on family night at the cinemas. It'd be hot, as long as everyone remembered that Millie doesn't like girls," Willow said, teasing her and making her giggle. Harvey began massaging her other foot, and Willow swapped Millie onto her other breast.

"What do you think, baby?" Harvey asked Millie.

"Do you want Mama all the time?" He added but already knowing the answer by Millie's excitedly giggles and nodding head.

"Yes please, Daddy," she said her hands coming up to play with Willow's tits.

"Right then. I guess we can give it a go and see how it works for a month or so," Harvey said surprised at how his life had turned upside down by the two women in front of him. He thought back to how simple life had been before Willow and Millie but quickly decided that what he had now was far better.

Chapter 10

Harvey watched as the two women began to over-run his house, finding it strange that he enjoyed them and their noise, their make-up covering his bathroom counter and their constant giggling. They had all seamlessly meshed their lives together, surprising him at just how easy it had been. He had heard the stories of people who had tried to do this, and it had all ended terribly. With one person feeling left out or jealousy rearing its ugly head and yet here they all were, eating breakfast on a Saturday morning after a week of work and meetings.

"Pass Mama the milk, baby girl," Willow said to Millie who had been given her coloring in book after she finished her fruit platter first. Millie held a fist full of pens in one hand, as she reached for the jug, just for Harvey to place his hand on it first.

"She's too little to lift it, Will," Harvey said causing Willow to raise her eyebrow over her reading glasses.

"Too little to follow Mama's direction, I don't think so," Willow said taking Millie's chin in her hand and shaking her head slightly before accepting the jug from Harvey. Harvey just laughed.

"She was last night," he said remembering how they had both fucked Millie until she couldn't stand without her legs buckling and when Willow had tried to make her, she had to catch Millie every time she tried.

"Well yes, she was," Willow said, standing up and kissing Millie gently on her lips before looking down at her drawing.

"Are you drawing a cute picture for Mama?" Willow asked, letting her hand casually grope Millie's tits over the top of the fluffy yellow sweater Harvey had dressed her in. Millie just giggled and squirmed as she was felt causing Willow to lick her lips at Harvey playfully before going into the kitchen.

"I'm going for a run, did you have any plans today?" Willow asked coming back with a sippy cup with water for Millie and a coffee for Harvey. He waited for her to place it in front of him before playfully grabbing her hips and pulling her onto his lap, making her laugh.

"You fool," Willow laugh slapping his chest but settling on his lap gently rocking her hips, enjoying how she felt him between her thighs.

"No, we do need to get the last of Millie's things from her house though. Maybe we can go to dinner after we do that?" Harvey suggested before getting kissed passionately, Millie looking up beaming at how lustful they were for each other. She loved having both of their affection and had found it interesting that she wasn't jealous of Willow. *Maybe it's coz I'm their baby as if I'd get jealous of Mama;* she thought to herself watching as Willow slipped her tongue into Harvey's mouth and sucked it sensually.

"Sounds good to me. See you soon, baby,"

Willow said, getting up as she copped a firm slap on her ass from Harvey and grabbed Millie's hand as she tried to slap her ass as well.

"Oh cheeky baby," Willow said, flicking her hand away and making Millie giggle as she sucked her paci and continued to color.

"Let's tidy up while Mama is gone baby girl," Harvey said as Millie started to become fussy. She had been kept in her high-chair for the last hour, and Harvey knew that she needed to get down soon. He carefully unlocked her, feeling her between her thighs as he placed her down on the floor.

"Stay there," he said suddenly, his voice desperate with lust. Millie watched as he disappeared, just to return with a thick vibrator and chastity belt.

"Oh, no, Daddy. I don't wanna," Millie said, trying to slap his big hands away.

"Shh little one, Daddy doesn't care what you want. This is what I want, so it's happening," Harvey said, lubing the toy with his spit and pinning Millie down with his thigh while the other held her legs apart.

"Daddy likes his little girl filled; you know that don't pretend you don't like it," Harvey plainly said pulling the top of Millie's diaper down and stuffing her with the toy making her squeal as it forced its a way inside her. Turning it on, Harvey watched as Millie's nipples went hard under her sweater. He had denied her ever to wear a bra in the house and liked the easy access she was forced to accept as he held one hand to her pussy holding the toy in place and reached under her sweater to flick and tease her nipples.

"Daddy likes you ready to be fucked," Harvey said, taking the belt and effortlessly pulling it up Millie's thighs as she felt her pussy start to relax around the toy inside of her. He locked it in place as a wicked smile spread across his lips.

"Tell Daddy which hole is still free to be fucked," Harvey whispered in Millie's ear as he placed her on his lap and bent her forward.

"My ass, Daddy," Millie said, worried that he

would try and fuck her there next.

"That's right little one, remember that. That if you are a naughty girl for Daddy, that's where my cock is going to go and stay for a while when we watch cartoons later," Harvey said grabbing her hips and roughly dry humping her ass making himself hard. Standing up, he just laughed as Millie whimpered and stayed on the floor as he began to tidy up from breakfast, his cock hard in his grey sweat pants.

"Did you turn Daddy on again little girl?" Willow said coming back from changing into her work out gear. She walked over to where Millie was standing and raised an eyebrow as she saw her baby belted and horny.

"We were just playing, weren't we Millie?" Harvey teased, jerking his cock. Willow came to sit next to Millie on the floor and swooned as Millie crawled to her, resting her face in Willow's deep cleavage, her sports bra making the top of her tits push out of her singlet.

"I know what you want baby girl, but Mama

likes you like this too so you'll have to be a good girl and stay like that until I get back. Here," Willow said, pulling her tit out and pushing Millie's mouth to her nipple. Millie grabbed Willow with both hands and suckled greedily, feeling the vibrator buried in her cunt make her clit throb. Willow held Millie's face close and pulled her into her arms as she nursed, waiting until Millie had settled and closed her eyes before gently taking her off.

"Be a good girl for Daddy, Mama will be back soon," Willow said lovingly to Millie who just nodded her head as Willow pushed her paci back in her mouth.

"Have fun," Willow called knowingly as she closed the door behind her.

Harvey had indeed had his fun with Millie before Willow had come back. They had painted, made cookies and Millie had helped with the washing before Harvey had taken her to the nursey they had all made and tied Millie to the wall.

"You aren't being punished little girl; Daddy just wants to make sure that you don't go anywhere while I work. Here, have your toys and be a good girl," Harvey said as he placed Millie's favorite stuffies in front of her and watched as she began to play.

Harvey walked down the hallway and into his room, lay on his bed, and sighed. He had never thought his life would turn out like this. *Having two women to fuck at my command, given I always have to ask Willow first, but she never says no, and Millie*, he thought reaching down to touch himself. She had been the perfect baby. Easy to train, easy to please, always willingly and so beautiful. Willow had dyed the tips of Millie's blonde hair purple, and it matched her deep blue eyes perfectly. Her skinny frame making him crave to touch her on sight, and he loved how open she had been to all his suggestions. *Is this just life now? This perfect fucking life with these two amazing women. I'm one lucky bastard*; he laughed to himself as Willow stormed into the room.

"Hey," Harvey said startled to be interrupted.

"Why is my little girl chained to the wall?" Willow said stripping, her body sweaty from her run, her hair messy like she'd just been fucked.

"I just needed a minute and didn't want her to run away," Harvey said, standing up and walking to Willow who placed her hand on his chest.

"Down boy, Mama isn't in the mood," Willow said, taking Harvey by surprise.

"If you were my little one I'd make you take a pounding for that," Harvey said, grabbing her hips and grinding his bulge into her pussy.

"But I'm not am I?" Willow teased, laying on the floor and beginning to play with herself. Harvey sat at the edge of his bed and shamelessly began jerking himself off at the sight of the powerful women fucking her pussy.

"I have an idea for Millie," Willow said breathlessly as she slid a finger into her cunt, gasping as it reached her hilt. Harvey knew what she was feeling, his cock had felt it countless times, and he closed his eyes, remembering how tight she was there.

"Yeah, what?" He groaned as he felt his orgasm building.

"I can't tell you," Willow said, making Harvey frown.

"Why not?" He almost yelled, standing up as he pumped his cock.

"Because your cock is about to be in my mouth," Willow said, opening her mouth and sticking out her tongue. Harvey excitedly straddled her face, pushing his cock down her throat and feeling her gag around his tip as he shot into her.

"Fuck yeah," Harvey groaned as he pumped Willow's mouth with his load shuddering as she swallowed him deeply.

"Finish me," Willow said when Harvey finally pulled his cock from her throat. He just laughed as he went to his cupboard and took out a paddle before leaving the room.

"Son of a bitch," Willow said, laying her head down on the floor and played with herself again, closing her eyes only to open them again as Harvey came back into the room.

"Baby," Willow said in surprise, reaching out to Millie who still had her diaper on.

"You're going to play with Mama until she's happy, baby girl," Harvey instructed unlocking her belt and reaching into her diaper. He roughly pulled the toy from Millie's pussy, making her squeal which just made Willow rub her clit harder.

"Come to Mama, baby girl," Willow said lovingly. Harvey reached her first, shoving the wet toy into her cunt and making Willow arch her back as the intruder made her cum instantly. She grabbed Millie's hand and held her back as her orgasm ravaged through her.

"No, baby," Willow said, making Millie confused. Willow let her climax die back down before she spoke again. Harvey had ripped Millie's diaper off and was busy slamming into her pussy as Willow held her wrist to the floor.

"Bring her here," Willow said breathlessly as Harvey reached down to pin Millie's head on the floor as he emptied inside of her. When he was finished, Millie got up and crawled to where Willow was patting her lap and wrapping her arms around Millie's younger body; Willow began nursing her as Harvey came back for more.

"Daddy's not finished," Harvey said lifting Millie's leg and fucking her as she lay cradled on her side in Willow's arms. Willow knew Millie was near her limit by the pained wincing and squeaks she was making around her nipple.

"Be gentle, Daddy," Willow said, eyeing him warningly as he slowed his onslaught. Millie curled her arms into her chest as Willow held her tight, forcing her to suckle as she was power fucked by Harvey.

"Red, red," Millie said suddenly, pushing Willow away as Harvey pulled out instantly, his cum spilling out onto the wooden floor.

"Millie are you ok, tell us what's going on," Harvey said, dropping to his knees and holding out his hand to Millie.

"It just hurt too much, I was playing, and then this and it was all just too much," Millie said as tears began to roll down her face. Willow bit her bottom lip and ran her fingers through her hair before she stood up.

"Hey come on sweetie, let's get you cleaned up and settled," she said, taking Millie into the shower. Harvey followed and watched as Willow took the lead and clean Millie's cum covered body, gently rubbing her pussy clean as Millie cuddled into her.

"I'm proud of you for saying red Millie," Harvey said lovingly as he reached out to touch her cheek. Millie just sighed as she rested her head in Harvey's hands while Willow finished washing her body.

"Thanks, Daddy. I'm happy you're not mad," Millie sleepily said.

"I could never be mad sweetheart," Harvey said as he helped Willow take Millie from the bath. He wrapped her big pink fluffy towel around her and picked her up as he carried her to the living room.

"Where do you need to be Millie," Willow said stroking Millie's hair and offering Millie her paci. Millie just nodded her head and opened her mouth for Willow who pushed her paci past her pink lips.

"Take her to the nursery, Daddy," Willow said before going to the kitchen to heat a bottle.

"There you go little one," Harvey said, placing Millie onto the changing table and beginning to diaper her. He sprinkled fresh powder over her and rubbed it in gently before seeing Willow return with Millie's blankie and bottle. He closed the tabs and pulled on her safari onesie before picking her up again and taking her to the rocking chair. Sitting down, he cradled her in his arms as Willow placed the blanket on top of Millie and passed the bottle of Harvey.

"You're a good girl, next time we play we will make sure you're a big girl first, ok baby?" Willow said, placing her hands on her hips and watching her lover.

"I'm sorry Daddy hurt you, baby," Harvey said, bringing Millie up to his lips to kiss her face gently before continuing to rock her to sleep. As her bottle emptied, and her eyes grow tired, Harvey carried her to the crib and lowered her down.

"See you in a little while baby," he said to a sleeping Millie before leaving the room and shutting the door behind him.

"Fuck," Willow said as she saw Harvey walk into the living room. Willow had finished off tidying the house and was reading a magazine while she waited for Harvey to return.

"Right!?" Harvey said, sitting down next to her. They both sat in silence and listened to the birds outside.

"I mean, we do fuck her like she's a slave," Willow said, turning to face Harvey.

"Yeah, I know. I feel so bad," Harvey said his eyes growing wide and shaking his head.

"Same. Has she ever stopped it before?"

Willow asked.

"No never, usually I catch her before she goes over the edge but, not this time," Harvey said, annoyed at himself.

"What do you need?" Willow said, seeing how disappointed he was with himself. He looked up at her curiously.

"What?" He asked, unsure of what she was meaning.

"Well, we just looked after Millie, but she's not the only one who is feeling shit. Do you need to go for a walk or be reminded that you are a great man and such a loving Daddy?" Willow suggested making him laugh.

"I don't feel so great right now," he said, leaning forward and putting his hands on his knees.

"Let's look at the facts. You stopped the minute she needed to when you were like mid-orgasm. You took the time to look after her and get her back into a good space and are giving her what she needs. You're ok; she still thinks you are amazing," Willow said, placing her hand on his back.

"What about you?" Harvey asked, turning his head to look at her.

"What about me?" Willow asked, confused.

"Well, don't you feel bad too?" Harvey asked, sitting up to look at her.

"Yeah I do, but she's not the first girl who has said stop to me, in fact, I get it a lot. I have already gone through my; I don't know, Dom drops if you like and I know that everything will be fine. You've just never had a girl you like fucking so much, so you've never felt this before. But it's ok, it's all going to be ok Harvey," Willow said, hugging him.

Chapter 11

"Daddy," Millie called from the nursery a few hours later. Harvey hadn't realized that he had fallen asleep until Millie's voice calling his name woke him. Getting up, he hurried to her side only to see her smiling up at him.

"Hi, there sweetie, did you have a good nap?" Harvey said, picking her out of the crib and holding her in his arms. Millie just nodded as she snuggled into him and felt his heart beat against her face.

"Daddy, can we go out like we did before," Millie said as Harvey walked her into the kitchen and made her lunch.

"Like, when you came home from work and went to a bar before being Daddy's little diapered princess?" Harvey teased, making her blush.

"Yeah," Millie said, taking the spoon and feeding herself the pumpkin soup Harvey had heated up for her.

"Yeah, sure. You'll still be Daddy's baby, though. Do you want to go just us or take Mama with us?" Harvey said as Willow came into the house with the last of Millie's things. She had gone out to collect the remaining three bags of Millie's clothes from her home. They had found people to rent the house out too and Millie had been excited that she'd be earning money as a landlord.

"Take Mama where?" Willow said, catching the end of the conversation.

"Nowhere, Mama," Millie said, going back to eat her soup. Harvey looked at her and hoped that their world wasn't falling around them. Willow just raised her eyebrows and continued down the hall to Harvey's room.

"Let's keep it a secret and take Mama out to something special, Daddy," Millie quickly said before Harvey could ask her if everything was alright, relieving his anxiety.

"Oh, ok that sounds like a fun idea," Harvey said whispering with matching excitement.

"Yeah, but I want to be a big girl for that night please, Daddy?" Millie asked, making Harvey lick his lips with excitement.

"Sure thing," he said, his eyes sparkling with the curiosity of what Millie was planning.

Millie had been swamped with work all week, working well into the night from Monday to Friday. With the plan for everyone to meet at 7:30, Millie knew she would be late.

"Hello little one," Willow said, answering Harvey's phone. She was just sliding her freshly pedicured feet into her black patent heels.

"Hey, um, I might be a little late, I'll be there by eight though ok?" Millie said, making Willow laugh.

"Oh baby, are you in your big girl office working hard? Can't you call me Mama because someone might learn that you are my little princess?" Willow teased making Millie blush. She felt a shiver run through her body as she heard Harvey in the background.

"Hey, baby, you on your way?" Harvey said, taking the phone off Willow.

"I just told, um, Willow, that I'll be like 30mins late. I just really need to get this stuff sorted," Millie said. Harvey paused before he spoke again.

"I don't know who you are talking about. Is it Mama?" Harvey said, the smile he tried to suppress spreading across his face and escaping his voice.

"Don't," Millie said with a warning in her voice.

"Or what baby? You'll tell Daddy off?" Harvey said, enjoying the discomfort he was putting Millie in.

"Say it. Say, Daddy; I'm going to be late," Harvey said aggressively. Millie held her breath and swallowed hard. Looking around the office, Millie saw one or two colleagues still typing on their computers and bit her bottom lip.

"I know you think you're a big girl, but you're still mine, and I've told you what I expect,"

Harvey said, sitting down on the couch. Willow came to sit beside him and placed her hands on his lap, resting against his large muscular body.

"I can't," Millie said, begging to be let off this once. Harvey put her on speaker and stared at Willow excitedly.

"We are waiting for you little one," Willow teased, both laughing as Millie groaned down the phone.

"I'll be late, Daddy," Millie said quietly, bending down to speak under her desk.

"What about Mama, you were rude to her as well," Harvey said zipping up Willow's black dress.

"Mama, I'm sorry," Millie said, her voice breaking and her little voice escaping. Millie burned red as she sat back up, hoping that no one had heard her.

"You don't even know how sorry you're going to be," Harvey said, taking the phone and ending the call before Millie could reply.

"Too harsh?" Harvey asked Willow who

was pouring herself a red wine.

"No, fuck her, the rude little bitch," Willow said, her heels sounding loudly against the slate floors.

"Oh, we will," Harvey said, offering his hand to her as they headed to the door.

Millie knew she was fucked. Mostly because it was 8:45 by the time she reached the bar, and Harvey's promise to punish her loomed over her head. Walking into the bar, Millie smiled as the smell of beer hit her. She took off her coat and placed it on the hook by the door as she let her eyes wander. The room was dark, men in suits drank the week's problems away, and she watched as they drank scotch straight. Smelling the familiar smell of Harvey's cologne, Millie turned around smiling.

"Hi Daddy," she said upon seeing him. He had dressed in his signature heavy dark denim jeans. His slight pink oxford button down had the sleeves rolled up. *Only a very tough man can pull that off*, Millie thought as he held her like she was the most precious thing in the world. He had got his lines and fade away touched up, and he had worn his large platinum ring on the middle finger of his left hand and his watch on his right wrist. Releasing Millie from the bear hug he had held her in, he took in her appearance, enjoying that she had made sure her make-up was fresh. Her black, high-waisted business skirt was tucked into her emerald green lace blouse. Harvey could see that she had worn her black lace bra underneath and had taken the black singlet that he had handed her that morning off. Her hair tumbled down both sides of her face, and her baby blues stared at him with all the innocence in the world.

"See something you like, Daddy?" Millie teased, pushing into him as she passed and went to greet Willow.

"Someone was a naughty girl," Willow whispered in Millie's ear as she held her, biting her ear roughly until Millie pulled away in pain.

"I'm sorry, Mama," Millie tried to say but had Willow's hand covering her mouth before she could finish.

"Did I say I fucking wanted to hear your reasons for being a disrespectful little bitch?" Willow said, sitting back on the bar lounge and crossed her long legs, flicking her foot up and down as her eyes burned holes into Millie.

"I should have you down on your fucking knees right here begging for my forgiveness," Willow said as she slid her glass along the table.

"Get me a drink, that'll be a good start," Willow added, staring at Millie. Millie got up, taking the glass in her hand before walking to the bar where Harvey was waiting.

"So, that went well, I'm assuming?" He laughed, taking a sip of his beer. Millie just looked at him with her big puppy dog eyes.

"Don't look at me like that, baby, you did it to yourself," he said, paying for the drinks and walking back to where Willow was sitting.

"How was your day?" Millie asked Harvey as he sat with his arm around her and Willow. Willow had placed her hand on his thigh and was slowing stroking him while she drank.

"Just the usual. A guy that I've been training for three years finally reached his goal weight, so that was awesome," Harvey replied, kissing the top of her forehead. Millie rested her head on Harvey's shoulder and sighed, the stress of the week finally lifting.

"Have you finished what you've been working on?" Willow asked, reaching her hand over to stroke Millie's cheek affectionately, her eyes softening as she felt Millie's soft skin.

"Yeah, finally. It was so crazy; everything just seemed to happen all at once. It's never been that busy before. But it's all sorted now so thank goodness," Millie explained sipping her drink slowly. Harvey held the glass to her lips and tipped the rest of it down her throat.

"Come on, let's get out of here," he said, smiling knowingly at Willow. Millie was confused; she had planned for them to stay for at least a few drinks.

"Well, since we had so much time to kill

while we waited for you, we've come up with a new plan," Harvey said taking Millie's hand and pulling her through the crowd of people who were now standing around the bar. He grabbed her coat and pulled her outside into the cold air of the night, making Millie's head feel dizzy. Harvey whistled for a taxi as Willow helped Millie put on her coat and wrapped her arm around her predatorily.

"Where to Sir?" The taxi driver asked as Harvey got in the car. Willow pushed Millie into the back seat and pulled her to her side as the car drove away.

"72 on Blackwood thanks," Harvey said smiling down into his lap.

"Mama, where are we going?" Millie asked. Willow was busy groping her tits underneath her coat before she bent her head and kissed Millie passionately.

"Don't ask questions slut," Willow whispered into the kiss, making Millie's eyes go wide with fearful anticipation.

The taxi driver pulled into an abandoned stockyard and Harvey tipped him generously and told him to be back there in four hours. Nodding, the man took the cash and drove away, leaving the three of them standing by the lamp post light.

"Well, you've been a bad girl Millie, and do you know what happens to bad girls?" Harvey said, grabbing her by her chin and shaking her head.

"No, Daddy," Millie said swallowing hard.

"You don't? You're not that stupid, think," Harvey grabbing a handful of her hair and dragging her behind him, making her stumble on her heels as he walked her to the door of a tall building.

"They get punished," Millie said softly, wincing as Willow slapped her ass.

"They get punished, Daddy," Willow corrected.

"Maybe we've been too nice to you little one, maybe you have forgotten that your ours and that you promised to be a good girl and follow our rules. Maybe we need to teach you a lesson,"

Willow said, continuing to spank Millie as she tried to escape Harvey's grip.

"Don't you fucking dare move," he instructed, holding Millie's throat in his other hand and gripped her firmly until she took the spanking Willow was giving her silently.

"Good girl," Willow hissed as Millie began to whine with each spank. Harvey opened the door to the warehouse and turned the light on, taking Millie and pushing her inside. Stumbling, she fell on her hands and knees but looked up to take in the room.

"Daddy, what is this place?" Millie asked, making Willow roll her eyes.

"Shut up," she aggressively said, pushing a ball gag into Millie's mouth and securing it before Millie could resist.

"Uncle Ben is in the, let's just say, import and export business. He said we could use his playroom tonight," Harvey said, picking Millie up and taking her to a flogging cross. Pressing her body quickly to the cross, he and Willow secured her wrists above her head and her ankles apart, before standing back to take in their handy work. Millie struggled against her restraints, only adding to their amusement. He ran his fingertips over her body, enjoying that her back was to them and that she couldn't see what was going to happen to her.

"Do you think you can escape?" Harvey whispered in her ear as he took the hem of her skirt and ripped it in half, pulling the ruined material off her body and exposing her bare ass.

"Oh you are a little slut," Willow said, suddenly bringing a leather whip down onto Millie's ass. Millie just gasped as Willow began her assault, only stopping to spank Millie with both her hands.

"You better not ever fucking forget my name again, do you understand me?!" Willow growled into Millie's ear before going back to whip her. Harvey had poured himself a whiskey and was sitting on a chair as he watched and waited.

"I think you missed a spot," he said when Willow was finished. Standing up, Millie could hear his unmistakable foot-steps coming up behind her and grew wet with excitement. Placing one hand on the back of Millie's neck, he brought his full hand down on the top of her thighs making her squeal in pain as his handprint left significant red marks on her soft skin.

"Oh, it appears I did, good thing Daddy is here, isn't it princess," Willow mocked as she took a tube of lube and squirted it into her hands. She knew Millie would be wet, but she also knew she wanted to fuck her raw tonight and began to rub her hard, sliding her fingers in without warning and fucked her roughly.

"She'll take it," Willow said to Harvey who kicked his boots off followed by his shirt. He walked behind the cross to look at Millie in her eyes and cupped her face with his hands, rubbing her cheeks with his thumbs lovingly as Millie felt something slide up and down her slit. Her eyes going wide, with fear as she saw Willow come to stand next to Harvey.

"Who could it be baby?" Harvey said as he

and Willow walked back around behind her and out of sight as the unknown man spread her open and shoved himself inside her. Groaning in relief as his dick grew inside her, he held her hips as he pulled himself out of her tight cunt. He liked that there was no other choice for her than to take his long slow strokes, feeling his balls fill and become full, squishing against her ass as he filled her again slowly, and holding himself inside of her, making her feel him.

"Bye baby, have fun," Harvey was suddenly saying in her ear as he patted her on the head, took Willow's hand and walked out of the room.

Chapter 12

"Yeah, oh god, yeah," Ben said as he thrust into Millie's dripping cunt. She had long since discovered who was fucking her as Ben had taken her down from the flogging cross after cumming for the second time. He had bound her to a swing, suspending her in the air and teased her, saying how Harvey had told him she liked to swing into cock as he positioned a fucking machine with a thick dildo behind her swinging her into it by gripping her hair in a fist, only keeping her still to stuff her mouth full of his soft fleshly cock and hairy balls. He held her there, getting spit roasted by the machine and his cock until she had sucked him hard again, covering her face with his cream as he came hard.

"Are you still wet, slut? Fuck I'm a good guy for giving a shit and not just fucking you raw like whores like you deserve," Ben said pulling his cock from her mouth and walking behind her, taking the machine from her pussy. He took the tube of lube and pushed the opening into her cunt, squirting carelessly, filling her with lube until it dripped from her.

"What a fucking mess," Ben said, slapping her sensitive cunt until she was wriggling away from his touch.

"Where the fuck do you think you are going, you're mine bitch, your Daddy didn't want to fuck a naughty bitch like you, so he gave you to me for the night, and we haven't even started yet," Ben said, taking a pair of scissors and holding Millie still as he began to cut her blouse and bra off.

"As if you'll need these, how am I supposed to clamp your big tits if you're all covered up trying to hide from me?" Ben said roughly grabbing her tits and pulling them down with his thick fingers, rolling her nipples between his thumb and index finger until Millie was moaning against her gag.

"Yeah I know you like that, aren't I good to

you," Ben said, walking to a drawer and taking out nipple clamps with a lightweight attached to them. Millie groaned in pain as he secured them to her nipples, jiggling her tits as he laughed at her struggle.

"Just wait till you've got a cock in you, then you'll feel them," Ben teased as he stuck a finger into her pussy and made her swing forward. Taking his finger back out, he ran it around her ass before pushing it inside of her.

"I need you lubed up bitch," Ben said as Millie felt him press a butt plug inside of her.

"Cute little bunny, I can see how Harvey forgets to discipline you, look how adorable you look," Ben said ruffling the bunny tail of the butt plug before abruptly sticking his cock back inside her lubed pussy making Millie give out a high pitched moan.

"Oh I see she's still disobedient, did I not tell you to shut the fuck up bitch?" Harvey's voice pierced through the room, and he grabbed her face with both hands and made her look up at him.

"I see you're still bad, let's try and fuck the naughty out of you then shall we?" Harvey sneered, taking out Millie's gag just to replace it with his hard cock and began to fuck her face.

"Well, I can see you boys are having fun," Willow said coming to stand to the side of Millie's bound body and grabbing a handful of Millie's thick booty, slapping it a few times as she looked at her being taken from both ends.

"Let me know when you're finished. I've got a special surprised for our naughty girl," she said casually as she began whipping Millie's back gently. Millie just swung between the two men, being plow until they were finished. Ben cumming over her ass crack and smiling as he saw his cum drip down to the plug and Harvey spilling from Millie's lips and making a puddle on the floor. Lazily slapping her cheek, Harvey pulled himself from her mouth and watched as Millie gasped for air before walking behind her and slapping her ass with his cock.

"You know what I like about this one?"

Harvey said to Ben, who was still standing behind her watching her body shake involuntarily.

"What I like is that she never says no the good little slut," Harvey laughed as he grabbed the swing and pulled Millie back and into his cock.

"Gag her, I don't want to fucking hear her," Harvey said to Willow who just rolled her eyes.

"It's alright, I've got it, open wide pretty girl," Ben said, flopping his limp dick into Millie's mouth.

"Suck it you lazy bitch," Harvey said slapping Millie's ass and getting turned on watching it shake.

"Yeah, that's it," he added, slapping her over and over as he pounded her from behind.

"She likes it, she's not even trying to fight it anymore," Ben laughed, pushing his balls into her mouth.

"Gobble it all up, and maybe your Daddy will give you a treat on the way home," Ben said, jerking his cock and slapping it against Millie's face. Harvey slapped her harder as he came, thrusting aggressively into her as he exploded balls deep in her.

"Enjoy," he said patting Ben on the shoulder as he passed, sitting down on the chair and yawning in satisfaction as he watched Ben face fuck, Millie. Ben finished again, this time holding Millie's nose closed, making her keep her mouth open as she tried to deny him.

"Nice fucking try slut," he just laughed as he filled her mouth before moving back to her cunt.

"Uh huh, my turn," Willow said, starring Ben down.

"She's all yours," he finally said, walking back to Millie's face and slapping her contently. He walked over to the other chair and sat down slowly and took out a box of cigars.

"Were they mean you, little princess? Do you remember what you fucking are now? You're ours, and we will give you all the lovies in the world, but step out of line and we will destroy you, pretty girl," Willow explained as she untied Millie's limp body. Willow helped Millie stand and lay her on the floor, taking a wet wipe and cleaning her before taking her hand and leading her to the king size bed that was set up in the corner of the room.

"Lay down for Mama," Willow said. Millie was in such a heightened headspace she silently obeyed, making Willow smirk.

"Whose little girl are you, baby," Willow said standing over the top of Millie.

"Yours, Mamas and Daddy's. And Uncle Ben's when you say," Millie said in a haze. Willow took her dress off slowly and waited for Millie to have an idea of what was coming next.

"You didn't think I was going to let them have all the fun, did you?" Willow said as she took the nipple clamps off Millie's sensitive body, making her gasp as she felt the blood flow back to them.

"Arms up," Willow gently said, waiting for Millie to obey her. Slowly, Millie raised her arms above her head, breathing shallowly as Willow tied her wrists to the bed frame.

"See, the boys like to play rough, but they

don't know something that Mama does. Do you know what is it?" Willow said, kissing down Millie's body and tying her ankles to the other end of the bed. Millie just shook her head no as Willow began to lovingly stroke her stretched body, enjoying how the bones of Millie's ribs and pelvis pushed against her skin.

"I didn't think you would. It's this, that the more gentle you are with your toys, the longer it takes to break them, the more they love you, and the easier it is for you to be in their head controlling them long after you have stopped touching them," Willow said as she began to rub Millie's pussy making her gasp with surprise.

"Yeah, Mama is going to fuck you. It doesn't matter if you find it hot or not, you're mine, and I want you tonight. Are you going to be a good girl for me and stay quiet?" Willow asked Millie as she rubbed her. Millie moved her hips in time with Willow's touch, breathing in ragged gasps as she felt Willow creep slowly into her head in a way Harvey and Ben didn't seem to be able to. Closing her eyes, Millie whimpered as Willow rubbed her clit gently, her mind beginning to crave the sound of Willow's voice. Licking her lips, Willow bent down to kiss Millie's nipples and tits, Millie opening her eyes as she felt Willow slide two fingers inside of her.

"Shh, we don't want the others to hear, do we? What would they think, they wouldn't understand would they baby? You'll get me in trouble when all I'm doing is making you feel good. It does feel good, doesn't it? I want to make you feel good, beautiful," Willow whispered in Millie's ear as her body pressed against her, the weight of her breasts pressing onto Millie's lungs while her fingers moved inside her, building her orgasm.

"Are you going to be a good girl and cum for me?" Willow said kissing Millie's lips, biting them and making Millie moan and softly whine. Willow kept her soft, gentle pace as Millie started to buck her hips against Willow's hand, grinding down as her orgasm rocked her body.

"There's my good girl, shh shh, it's ok,

you're safe with me, you're always safe with me little one. Cute, you've made a mess. I like making your little body shake like that," Willow said, wrapping her arms around Millie and holding her tight as Millie hyperventilated.

"I've never done that with a girl before," Millie softly said, pulling on the ties that secured her wrists, panicking slightly.

"Woman. I'm a woman, baby. Shh don't frown, sweetie, you don't want to get wrinkles on this beautiful little face, let me," Willow said stroking Millie's forehead until she stopped frowning. After untying her wrists, Willow pulled the sheets of the bed back and climbed in with Millie cuddling close.

"Such a pretty, skinny, good girl. God, you are stunning with these big titties and little body," Willow said softly touching Millie as Millie began to cautiously explored Willow's body, making her smile and move, to give Millie better access.

"You don't know what to do, do you baby?" Willow said, finding it endearing that Millie was so nervous. Millie just shook her head and began blushing, looking down and trying to avoid Willow's gaze.

"Here, let me show you. Do it like this," Willow lovingly said, taking Millie's hand in hers and making her touch her pussy, laughing when Millie pulled her hand away swiftly.

"Don't be so shocked. Of course, I'm wet for you sweetie, look at you, you're what dreams are made of, with your beautiful little face and fuck-able body," Willow said, gently taking Millie's hand and placing it back to her pussy and running a finger up and down her slit. Millie watched nervously as Willow used her hand on her cunt, making Millie rub her clit firmly.

"Yeah baby, that's it, good girl," Willow said in gasps, pulling Millie's body across hers and rubbing her clit again, making Millie gasp but just rock in her arms. Willow pushed her nipple into Millie's mouth as she gently fucked her, enjoying feeling Millie's gasps and moans on her big breasts, sending vibrations through her body.

"Do you want to feel inside baby?" Willow asked as she forced herself to rub Millie slowly instead of the power fuck she wanted to give her.

"Come on sweetie you've been such a good girl for me, don't disappoint me now," Willow said patting Millie's pussy and cupping her gently as she kissed her forehead. Millie just nodded her head and held her breath as she slid a finger inside Willow, making her sigh with relief.

"Good girl, and another one sweetie," Willow instructed. Millie tenderly pushed another finger inside the older woman, feeling her tighten against her fingers.

"Move them like I am baby," Willow said as she began to wiggle her fingers inside of Millie, causing her to whimper as she copied.

"Don't stop baby, don't stop till I take your hand away, ok?" Willow groaned, fucking Millie harder as her orgasm hit her. Surprised that she had cum so quickly, Willow kept fucking Millie until she was a squirming mess on top of her as Millie's orgasm ravaged her exhausted body.

"Good girl, I'm so proud of you," Willow said, taking Millie's hand away and licking her juices off Millie's fingers. Holding Millie's face with both hands as she rested on top of Willow's large tits, Willow looked into Millie's soul before smiling and kissing her deeply on the mouth. Millie wrapped her arms around Willow, flexing her back muscles as she was held by the older woman, getting so lost in the kiss she hardly heard Harvey clear his throat behind her.

"Ok, time to go," Harvey said, coming over and pulling the sheets off the bed in one fluid action. Millie just lay in bed, her mind racing, her body sore, her heart yearning. *What is that, what is that feeling?* Millie thought to herself as Harvey handed her a bag with spare clothes.

"You'll need to get dressed quickly, the taxi will be here soon," Harvey said. He had already showered and redressed and had been sitting with Ben smoking cigars. Millie looked at Willow and hated herself for what she felt.

"Will, I, Mama um can I sleep in your bed

tonight?" Millie stuttered, remembering not to call Willow anything but Mama, feeling lucky that the start of Willow's name was a word all on its own. Getting dressed Millie looked at Willow with an innocence she didn't know she could feel. Willow just smirked and winked at Harvey.

"No sweetie, you need to sleep in your bed. You don't love me, you just love feeling loved," she said, knowing that she had Millie hooked. Disappointed, Millie just nodded and walked out of the room and into the night air.

"Aren't you going to say thank you?" Ben said, standing up and following her outside.

"Whatever," Millie said back, a pain in her heart that she didn't understand.

"Whatever?!" Ben said, making Harvey stand up and storm out after her.

"I thought we'd taught you a big enough lesson but not!" He said, reaching out to grab her upper arm and turn her around before slapping her face angrily.

"Let me go! Stop, red, I'm done, I'm fucking

done," Millie said, pulling away from him and running into the night.

"What the hell did you do with her?!" Harvey yelled, running back into the room just as Willow picked up her coat.

"I loved her. While you two idiots were busy hate fucking her until she was so filled with your cum that her pussy dripped for hours, I was gentle; I took my time with her, I made her feel safe. Couldn't you see it, see her need to be held and treasured? Sure she could take cock like a champ, but couldn't you see she fell for you because of the way you made her feel precious? You lost her when you let him fuck her; you lost her when you didn't let her be your baby girl for longer than an hour without wanting your cock serviced. You changed with her just because she never made you wait. You stopped being her Daddy, Harvey and you know it. You just became some guy she let fuck her in exchange for a moment of your softness," Willow said. She pulled her coat tight across her chest as she walked

passed Harvey and Ben and towards the waiting
Taxi.

Chapter 13

Willow's words cut Harvey to the core because he knew she was right. He had changed. He had become obsessed with only one thing, how many times he could stick his cock inside her. He had walked the two-hour walk home the night Millie had run out on him, and it had been a month since he had seen her. She had come to pick up her things, moving back into her apartment the day after that night. Willow had moved out too, but to where, Harvey didn't know or particularly care. He had let them both down; he had let himself down. *Too much of a good thing hey*, he thought to himself as he repositioned a new client who had shamelessly flirted with him the whole training session.

Millie had come home early from work on a sunny afternoon to find Willow resting on her car bonnet, the fall sun making her raven hair even more beautiful.

"Hey," Millie happily gasped, seeing Willow outside her door.

"Hi," Willow replied, getting up and walking over to Millie.

"I'm not coming back this time. Willow, I can't," Millie said making it a point to say Willow's name.

"I know. I'm not here for that. I'm here to make sure you're ok," Willow replied as Millie stopped outside her door.

"Did Harvey send you?" Millie said, turning to face Willow. Their time together flashed through Millie's thoughts, and she had to shake her head, trying to shake them from her mind.

"No. Has he come to check on you?" Willow asked, putting her hands in her pockets. Millie just shook her head no.

"Cold. He should have. Look, I'm sorry it all ended like it did. I hope you know not all Daddies are like that. He used to be awesome, I don't know what happened, but I'm sorry he turned into something cold with you. You didn't deserve that," Willow said, making Millie smile.

"I never thought I'd hear you say all that," she said shocked that Willow was so honest with her.

"Well it's true so," Willow said watching as the clouds moved over the sun. Millie looked at her and smiled, thinking of how she had changed in the time she had known Willow.

"Look, it's fin. Honestly, I'm seeing another guy at the moment, and I'm starting to see the differences," Millie said, looking down at the ground.

"Oh, nice. That's great. So no women?" Willow said cheekily making Millie roll her eyes and laugh.

"No, I'm not gay, I keep telling you that. I just liked you. But that was a different time and different place so," Millie said, trailing off as the sun came back from behind the clouds.

"Thanks for everything Will, it was, one hell

of a crazy ride," Millie said, stepping forward and kissing Willow more passionately than Willow was ready for. Taking her hands out of her pockets, Willow held Millie as they kissed.

"Bye Willow," Millie said, unlocking the door to her house. Willow nodded and looked at Millie lovingly as she walked into her house and shut the door behind her. Millie stayed leaning against the door as she breathed deeply, Willow's perfume still in her nose. Sam just looked at her and smiled. He had seen the kiss and pieced together the faces from the stories Millie had told him.

"That was her, wasn't it?" Sam said, coming over to take Millie's bag from her shoulder.

"Yeah, it was," Millie said, content with the closure she just experienced. Sam smiled at her and took her hand, leading her into the kitchen.

"I've made you two types of snacks because I didn't know which one you'd want more. There's honey sandwiches or cheese and crackers," he said, bringing over Millie's sippy cup.

"And of course, juice," he laughed as he placed the cup in Millie's clapping hands.

"Thank you, Daddy," she said as Sam began to take her shoes off.

Who is Tina Moore?

Tina Moore has enjoyed the lifestyle of a Mommy Domme for several years. She began exploring kink and BDSM in her youth and found her love of being a strict Mommy Domme in early 2000. Tina Moore is now an author of many MDLG, DDLG and ABDL themed novels.

Follow her on:

Author Page on Amazon

Instagram @tinamoore.kdp

www.ingramcontent.com/pod-product-compliance
Lightning Source LLC
Chambersburg PA
CBHW031019190726
48286CB00003BA/919